WALK MY WAY

BOOKS BY PAIGE DIXON

Lion on the Mountain
Silver Wolf
The Young Grizzly
Summer of the White Goat
The Loner: A Story of the Wolverine
Promises to Keep
May I Cross Your Golden River?
Skipper
The Search for Charlie
Pimm's Cup for Everybody
Walk My Way

Walk My Way

by Paige Dixon

Atheneum 1980 New York

To Katherine Sharp
who looked after us all so well

LIBRARY OF CONGRESS CATALOGING IN PUBLICATION DATA

Walk my way. Dixon, Paige.

SUMMARY: Attempting to flee from her problems, 14-year-old Kitty sets off into the wilderness determined to hike 50 miles from her New Hampshire home to the Maine village where her Aunt Lee lives. Her adventures give her the maturity and understanding to face her problems squarely.

I. Title.

PZ7.C814Wal [Fic] 79-23291

ISBN 0-689-30738-1

Published simultaneously in Canada by
McClelland & Stewart, Ltd.
Manufactured by Fairfield Graphics,
Fairfield, Pennsylvania
Designed by M. M. Ahern
First Edition

WALK MY WAY

CHAPTER ONE

THE LITTLE New Hampshire town had a closed-for-the-winter look. Labor Day was six weeks in the past, and the summer cottages down on the lake were boarded up. The grocery store at the head of the lake had taken down its sign, POP TAYLOR'S GROC., PERIODICALS, SUNDRIES, and the only store still open was the one the towns-people used, Roy's, across the street from the town hall and next door to the White Mountain Bar. A cold wind was blowing down the maple leaves that a few tourists were still coming to gaze at. It rattled the old windows in the town hall and chased a cloud of dust along the road.

"We need rain," Harry of Harry's Exxon Station said to the stranger who had driven up in the big station wagon that had a wired barrier between the driver and the back.

"Feels more like snow," the man said. He got out and stretched.

"Ain't cold enough for that." Harry peered at the small red-gold dog in the back, who returned his stare.

"Hey, what kind of dog is that?"

"Basenji."

"Come again?"

"Basenji. African Barkless, some call 'em. Very old breed, goes back to the old Egyptians, they tell me."

"Yeah? Pretty little fella."

"I drove two hundred miles to get him. I want him for a stud. There's good money in basenjis."

Harry twiddled his fingers on the glass, but the dog just looked at him with oval brown eyes outlined in black. "Uses mascara." Harry laughed, but the dog's unusual face, with the wrinkled brow and the large erect ears, made him a little nervous. "He looks at you the way a person does."

"They're smart." The man counted out the money he owed Harry. "Any place in this burg where I can get a drink?"

Harry's friendliness diminished at the slur to his town. "Across the street," he said shortly. "Joe Bellows'."

In Joe Bellows' White Mountain Bar, Kitty LeBlanc put her face to the glass of the door and said, "Looks like a customer. Station wagon, Massachusetts plates." Kitty washed dishes and did odd chores for the Bellowses after school. She was fourteen, nearly six feet tall, and broad-shouldered.

"Kitty, you're breathing all over the glass that I just Windexed," Mrs. Bellows said sharply.

Kitty pulled back quickly. "Sorry. I'll Windex it before I go home, Mrs. Bellows."

"The kid's got to breathe somewhere," Joe Bellows said, trying to turn it into a joke.

"Not on my clean glass." Mrs. Bellows flounced into the kitchen, and Kitty and Joe exchanged looks.

"She's had a hard day," Joe said.

"Sure. My fault anyway."

"Damn it, don't always say it's your fault, kid. You've got a right to live and breathe on this planet same as anybody else."

Kitty laughed. "Not to hear my pop tell it." She had a deep, strong voice, older than her years.

The door was shoved open, and the man who drove the station wagon came in. He looked Kitty over as she disappeared into the kitchen. "That's a big barmaid you've got there."

"What can I do for you?" Joe said, not returning the stranger's grin.

Undaunted by Joe's lack of response he said, "Tell you the gospel truth, I'd rather the lady waited on me."

"You'll have to settle for me," Joe said. "What'll it be?"

The man pretended to shiver. "Winter sets in early around here. A double Scotch. Black and White." He waited for the drink. "You fellows always so unfriendly?"

"Not unfriendly. Cautious."

The man laughed. "Fair enough." He winked at Joe. "Maybe got the young lady lined up yourself, hey?"

Joe put both palms on the bar and leaned toward the man. "Mister, the young lady is fourteen years old."

The man's eyes widened. "You're kidding! No, I guess you aren't. Say, that's one big girl. Jeez, what'll she be like at eighteen?" He raised his hand. "No offense, brother, no offense. She your kid?"

"No," Joe said, and turned away, polishing some glasses.

"Figured not. I mean you being kind of a little fellow." When Joe didn't answer, the man shrugged and gave his attention to his drink.

The silence was broken only by the sound of someone in the back washing dishes, but in a few minutes a low, quiet voice began to sing, almost inaudibly at first, but then increasing in volume, as if the singer had forgotten the surroundings and thought only of the song. It was a spiritual, "Deep River."

"Somebody sings real good," the stranger said.

"Somebody does."

"Sounds like that colored woman that used to sing songs like that . . . what was her name? Not Aretha Franklin, but . . ."

"Marian Anderson."

"Yeah, that might be the one." He finished his Scotch and put his money on the counter. "That's real pretty." He hesitated a moment at the door, then went out. He got into his car and started up the country road that connected with the interstate. It was getting dark. He slowed for a dirt crossroad, saw nothing, and drove into the intersection. A pickup with no lights barrelled along the dirt road, put on its brakes with a screech, and crashed into the station wagon, broadside.

The wagon spun halfway around, and the man slumped over the steering wheel, dazed from a bump on his head. The back fender was crumpled, and the tailgate had sprung open. The dog, hurled onto his side, lay still a moment. Then, as he heard the voice of the other driver shouting, he saw that he could escape through the broken tailgate. Without a backward look he leaped onto the road and ran.

CHAPTER TWO

JOE swabbed down the bar with a damp cloth. He had spent fifteen years in the Navy, and he liked things shipshape. He smiled as he listened to Kit out there washing the dishes and really taking off on a Kathleen Ferrier song, from a recording he had given her. She had rough places in her voice yet, but she had a true ear, and a quality that you just didn't hear very often. Joe was a frustrated musician. He played the piano and the guitar by ear, and he spent so much money on records, it was a constant source of friction with his wife.

He glanced at the calendar behind him. It was over a month since he had sent those tapes of Kit's to his old Navy buddy, now in the music business in New York. Kit laughed and said they'd never hear, but he had faith in old Angelo, even though they had not been in touch for several years now. All he had asked for was Angelo's opinion and some advice about where she should study and how much it would cost. Joe had some of his pension stashed away where the Mrs. didn't know about it, and he was prepared to spend it on Kit's training. It would be ticklish, of course, not only because of the wife but because of Kitty's father. Hadn't paid any attention to his daughter, after his wife died, until she was old enough to keep house for him. Joe had a very low opinion of Clarence LeBlanc. Lazy lay-about who never worked an hour more than he had to, and Joe knew for a fact, although Kitty never mentioned it, that Clarence beat up on her.

He tensed at the sound of shattering glass. The singing stopped abruptly. His wife swore. He didn't need to hear her angry words to know that Kit had broken some glasses again. It was true she was clumsy; it took a kid a while to get coordinated.

His wife slammed her way into the front of the bar. Kitty stood behind her propping open the swinging door, looking scared and guilty. "I've had it!" Mrs. Bellows said loudly, as if she were addressing a roomful of customers. "I have had it up to here."

"I'm awful sorry," Kitty said. She looked at Joe with her dark eyes and made a small gesture with her hands as if to say "I've done it again."

"Come on, Janet." Joe put out his hand to his wife. "Don't have a conniption. It's just a glass or two."

Mrs. Bellows was a small woman, but she looked formidable as she pulled herself up and glared at him. "It is not a glass or two. It is five glasses."

"Oh, oh," Joe said. He tried to grin at Kitty, but she looked on the verge of tears. "So five glasses. Chalk it up to overhead."

"I've been chalking up that kind of overheard ever since Kitty came to work for us. I can't afford any more. If you remember, Joe, the contents of this bar were bought with my money."

"I remember all right," he said drily.

She turned to Kitty and spoke a little more quietly. "I'm sorry, Kitty. You just aren't cut out for this kind of work. When you're older and not so clumsy, come back and see us. I don't mean to be mean. It's just that we can't afford it." She rang open the cash register drawer and counted out twenty dollars. "Here's your pay."

"No, keep it," Kitty said. "To pay for all I smashed." She had her chin tucked down into the cowl neck of her sweater as if she were trying to hide.

"No way. You take it. I won't have folks saying I don't pay my help." She thrust the money into Kitty's hand and returned to the kitchen.

Kitty looked at the floor for a minute. Then she shoved the money into the small front pocket of her jeans and said, "Well, see ya."

Joe followed her out on to the steps. "Listen, Kit, don't worry. I mean everything'll be all right."

"I'm sorry I blew it."

"Ah, forget it." He dug his hand into his pocket and pulled out a crumpled bill. "You take this to tide you over."

"No, you've done enough, Joe."

"Take it. You can pay me back when you're a famous singer. And listen, as soon as I hear from my chum Angelo, I'll be in touch, all right?"

She shook her head. "That won't happen, but I do appreciate . . ." She broke off and swallowed, trying not to cry. He pushed the money into her hand, and she put it in her pocket without looking at it. Mrs. Bellows's voice called for Joe.

"We'll think of something." He went back in.

She stood a moment, and then as she went down the four wooden steps, she missed her footing on the bottom one and almost fell. Some boys standing on the corner laughed, and one of them called out, "Watch your step there, Shorty."

She ignored them and went along the road toward her house. Billy Barrows, who coached at the high school, stopped raking the leaves in front of his house and said, "Hi, Kit."

"Hi, Coach," she said, hoping he wouldn't feel like talking.

"Did you see that dog that ran down the street a little bit ago?"

"Dog? No."

"Yeah. Darndest thing. Looked like a miniature deer. Ran like a deer, too, with long springy leaps right through the meadow and down toward the lake."

"I didn't see it."

"Mabel says I'm hallucinating." He grinned, leaning on his rake. "All set for the game tomorrow?"

"Sure."

"Get plenty of sleep. See you tomorrow."

"Goodnight, Coach." She didn't feel like playing basketball tomorrow. She felt like getting in her boat and going down to the end of the lake. It was nice there with everybody gone. Nobody came around except the man who checked the cottages for security once a month.

She walked more slowly as she approached the three-room house where she lived with her father. He'd blow his stack when he heard she'd lost her job. Maybe she ought to think seriously about leaving home. She'd considered it, but it was a big step. She could easily pass for eighteen, but her father might get the cops after her. And to get a job, she'd need an I.D. Lately she'd thought about going back to Aunt Lee's. She could finish school and get an after-school job to pay her expenses. One thing that had kept her at home was her job with Joe. He was so good to her, she hated to quit on him, but now that was solved. She would have to think it all over again, very carefully. It would mean she would be on her own, in a way. And she wasn't sure she was ready for that.

The TV was blaring, so her father was home. She took a deep breath and walked up the path.

CHAPTER THREE

THE dog ran across a field purple with asters, jumped a fence with ease, stopped to circle a cat who raised her fur and spat at him just in case he meant trouble. He left her to her hostility and ran through tall grass in leaps, his head appearing and disappearing like the prow of a small boat in heavy weather. He stopped at a brook that had been full during the summer but was dwindling now to its winter trickle and drank the cold water, his large ears pricked forward to detect anything interesting. A man driving a truck up the dirt road from lake to town turned his head to look at him, and the dog sped away.

When he came to the shore of the lake, two small boys were digging for worms or just for general information, and when they saw him, they squealed and sat back on their heels.

"What's that?" the smaller boy said.

"A dog, stupid. Don't you know a dog when you see one?" Having recently learned to whistle, he whistled piercingly.

"Here, doggy, doggy." The smaller boy held out a grubby hand.

The dog, not quite a year old, was young enough still to enjoy a good game. He leaped close to the boys but just out of reach and crouched on his front legs. As the boys scrambled up, he pranced sideways. They gave chase, and he circled them, now and then stopping with his head down, peering at them, the furrow on his brow deeper than ever. It gave him an anxious look, but he was not anxious; this was fun.

"His tail's curly like a pig's," the small boy said.

"Well, he ain't a pig." The other boy pounced, and the dog sprang away and ran up a big pine tree as fast and agile as a squirrel. The boys stared at him with their mouths open. They looked at each other in wonder.

"Dogs don't climb trees."

The dog stretched comfortably along a branch and looked down at them with bright eyes.

"He's a cat, some weird kind of cat," the second boy said. "Lookit, he's washing his paws. Dogs don't wash their paws."

"Nobody's going to believe us," his friend said. They stood at the foot of the tree staring up at the dog until he leaped from the branch to the ground and ran off.

"Let's don't tell anybody," the older boy said. "My father would just say, 'Tommy, quit your lyin'.' "

"I won't tell," his friend said. "Maybe if we come

here tomorrow, he'll come back. We could bring some dog food."

"Or cat food." The boy giggled suddenly. "Or fish food or pig food or dinosaur food."

But when they came back the next day, the dog had already journeyed to the far end of the lake, had pushed open a back door that a careless cottager had left unlocked, and had found half a bag of dry dog food. The house was cold, and he shivered, for his coat was short, but he curled up on a mattress and slept undisturbed.

CHAPTER FOUR

KITTY had played a miserable game of basketball, and she knew it without the groans of the fans to remind her. She couldn't keep her mind on the game. For one thing, her closest friend Mick wasn't there. It was the first game of Kitty's that Mick had ever missed, but lately her mind was on Billy Mitchell, not on Kitty, and it hurt. And the night before when Kitty told her father that she had lost her job, he had told her at length what a burden she was, and how worthless. To make sure she got the point, he had hit her hard on the side of the head. After the grilling Joe Bellows had put him through, he knew enough to hit where the marks didn't show. But now twenty-four hours later, Kitty's ears still rang and her head ached. The other team members and the coach had been kind.

"Kit's so good, she's entitled to a bad day now and then," Coach Barrows had said, but she knew they were disappointed. She had let them down. As far as she could see, trying to look at it objectively, she let everybody down.

She fixed her father's supper and watched with relief when he went off with his drinking pal, Mort. Mort, a retired gandydancer, who lived alone in a shack near the railroad where he invested most of his pension in alcohol, was a bad influence, and usually she dreaded to see him show up, but this time she wanted to be left alone. Mort made his usual leering remarks to her, but she had learned to ignore him, except for a time or two when she had had to fight him off.

When they were gone, she cleaned up the place and lay down on her cot, trying to think. Two of her friends came, but she pleaded a headache, and after looking at her pale face, they left. They were good kids. She was glad they had stopped by. But they lived in what she called to herself 'normal houses' with normal parents who liked them, and brothers and sisters that they fought with but liked. The gulf between their situation and hers was too wide to bridge. They were protected.

She lay down again and thought about Aunt Lee. She had been loved and protected when she lived with Aunt Lee, but that had come to an end five years ago when her father came for her. Aunt Lee had cried, but there had been nothing she could do. She wasn't even Kitty's real aunt, just a close friend of Kitty's mother. Now, though, Kitty was nearly grown up. Legally he could still fight to keep her, but if she said how bad he had treated her, and Joe would be on her side. . . . She had not heard from Aunt Lee lately, but she usually wrote only at Christmas and birthdays and times like that. It was a comfort to know she was just fifty miles away in her little town on the Maine coast. Kitty wished she could talk to her. She couldn't say much in a letter, because her father would open the mail if he got to it first. She looked at the smiling snapshot of Aunt Lee that she kept in the drawer of the table by her bed, and thought, "She wouldn't even know me now." It depressed her. Maybe Aunt Lee wouldn't want such a great ox of a girl. Kitty got up and found some aspirin tablets and soon fell asleep.

It was nearly dawn when she was awakened by the noisy arrival of her father and Mort. They sounded thoroughly drunk. She heard the screech of bedsprings as her father collapsed onto his bed, and Mort's hoarse laugh. Quickly she got up and dressed. You never knew what would happen. The lock on the door was flimsy, but she turned the key anyway and waited, hoping Mort would go away. She heard him rattling the coffeepot, and in a minute he banged on her door.

"Kitty, hey, Kitty, wake up and make me some coffee."

She didn't answer. He banged harder. "I want some coffee pronto."

"Then make it," she said.

"Now, Kitty, that ain't friendly. Come on out." He rattled her doorknob. "I want to talk to you."

"Go home, Mort," she said. "It's almost daylight."

"Not till you make me some coffee."

"Then will you go?"

"Sure as shootin'."

She hesitated. She was not afraid of him. He was a skinny little fellow; the muscle he had once had now gone to flab. But she hated the embarrassment of the kind of scene he sometimes started, and she couldn't bear to have him touch her, even in a friendly pat on the shoulder. But maybe if she made the coffee, he would go and not make a fuss. She unlocked the door.

He staggered into the room and grabbed her. "That's a good girl. How about a nice mornin' kiss?"

She shoved him away from her, but he bounded back and seized her around the waist, throwing her off balance. She fell backward onto the cot, he on top of her. She got her hand under his bristly chin and shoved his head back, and then she pulled up her knee and kicked as hard as she could at his stomach. He let out a yell of pain and fell backward, hitting his head on the radiator. He didn't move.

Kitty stared down at him. Blood from the blow on the head began to trickle down his temple. His face was white. "My God," she said aloud, "I've killed him." She tried to make herself feel his pulse to see if he was alive, but she couldn't bring herself to touch him. "I've got to get out of here," she said. In a panic she thrust a few things into her old canvas backpack—a change of clothes, Aunt Lee's picture, a faded snapshot of her mother, her comb and toothbrush. Mort had not moved. She went out of the house silently and walked fast toward the lake where she kept her boat. The only place she could think of where she was unlikely to be seen was down at the end of the lake. From there to Aunt Lee's stretched fifty miles of mostly woods.

CHAPTER FIVE

Kitty got her boat out of the old boathouse that her friend Mick's father let her use and carried it down to the water's edge. It was an almost new kayak that Joe Bellows had sold her two summers ago for practically nothing because he had decided he wanted an Old Towne. It was Kitty's dearest possession. In the kayak she could get away from everything and enjoy the lake that she loved.

Now her one thought was to get out of sight. Dawn had already made pink and mauve streaks in the eastern sky, and in the distance she could hear the wheezy engine of the milk truck. She headed for the end of the lake, staying close to the southern shore where there were no cottages.

The lake was nearly three miles long, the last mile much narrower than the rest. Most of the shore was wooded, with cottages set among the trees, but the southern side had suffered a forest fire some years ago and had grown up now in scrub oak and new pines still no more than a few feet high. Close to the water for a mile or so there ran a narrow-gauge railroad track, long unused and strewn with weeds.

Kitty had a vivid memory of coming out here with her mother to a particularly luxuriant growth of high-bush blueberries. They would pick and pick the big juicy berries and drop some into the milk pail but eat most of them, until at last, hot and tired and happy, they would sit on the warm ground and laugh at each other's blue-smeared faces and fingers. When she remembered her mother, it was the laughter and the games and the bear hugs. "My Kitten," her mother called her. Her father had been different then, clean and neat, with a good job in the ticket office of the railroad. The accident that had killed her mother and hospitalized him for weeks had changed him completely. Sometimes it seemed to Kitty that it had scrambled his brains.

But she didn't want to think about that now. She didn't want to think either about Mort Jenkins lying on her bedroom floor, possibly dead, in any case badly hurt. What she had to think about was getting to Aunt Lee's. She wished she had thought to bring something to eat. She was always hungry. She had the money from the Bellowses, but she couldn't risk going to a store anywhere. "I'm so conspicuous," she thought, and dug her paddle deep into the water in frustration. She tried to remember whether they still had the death penalty in New Hampshire. Would it apply to minors? It would be better to be dead than shut up somewhere for life. She shivered.

The wind was rising, and there was a light chop on the water. A boat with an outboard motor appeared, coming up from the point where the lake narrowed. She paddled as close to shore as she could, hoping whoever it was would not see her, but when the boat passed her some distance out, the man held up his hand in the stiff wave of passing boatmen. She returned the wave. She didn't recognize the boat, and she prayed he didn't know who she was. The Fullerton cottage had been sold recently; perhaps it was the new owner checking up on his property before the lake froze over.

She paddled fast, with long rhythmic strokes. Even if he didn't know her, he might mention to someone that he had seen a girl in a little kayak, and everyone would know it was she. Although the air was chilly, her forehead broke out in sweat.

It seemed to take forever to get to the far end of the lake. The wind was against her, the water seemed to fight her; perhaps God was against her. But God, of all people, ought to know that she had not meant to hurt Mort, only to protect herself. It seemed to be always happening, some disaster resulting from her strength. She thought of the time she had accidentally killed a chicken someone had given her for Easter. She had picked it up to caress it, and in her enthusiasm she had killed it. She'd cried all day. The changes in her when she started to grow had come too fast; it was too hard to understand that she was a whole different person. Even now, when she could bear to look into a mirror, she had a sense of shock, of thinking, But that isn't me. But it *was* she, and she was stuck with it.

She let the kayak drift for a moment, close to shore, hunching up her shoulders to ease the muscles. As far as she could see, there was no boat on the lake now, and no one in sight on shore. She dipped the double-bladed paddle into the water again, and the light boat shot forward.

At last she came to her destination, the bend of the lake at its farthest end. Here there were several cottages, but she knew the owners, and she knew they had all gone back to the city. She eased the kayak alongside the rocks that lined the little cove at the Prentiss place. The dock had been taken in for the winter to avoid ice damage, and she had to reach up and catch hold of the iron rail above the rock wall. She let the boat rock in the gentle wake while she hoisted herself up and under the rail, and then she maneuvered the boat up out of the water until she could get her arm under it and lift it out. She turned it over on the pine needles and went to sit and think on the Prentiss's broad steps.

The two things she most wished for were a map and food. She knew the woods for some distance, but she of course did not know them all the way to Maine. A compass would help, but she had nothing. If the sun stayed out, that would simplify things a good deal. At the moment it was shining and the sky was clear.

She got up and walked around the cottage. The Prentisses were from Boston. She had baby-sat for them several times, and they were always very nice to her. She looked in one of the windows. What if they had left some food? They were young and sometimes not as careful about little things as the older cottagers. The usual thing was to take all food, even canned stuff, away in case it might freeze, but supposing they had overlooked something? Her stomach was so empty it hurt. But breaking and entering was a crime.

She walked slowly past the bedroom windows to the back. It was a crime, but if you were already a murderer, a bit of breaking and entering wouldn't make much difference, would it? If she took anything, she'd leave the money for it.

She stopped short. The back door was slightly ajar. She could hardly believe it. She wouldn't have to break in, she would only be entering. She could say to the Prentisses, "I saw your door open, and I checked to see if there were vandals . . ." No, she would never see the Prentisses again, and anyway they weren't the kind of people she wanted to lie to. She took a few steps toward the door and then ducked back. The door was opening from the inside. Fear made her breath stop in her throat. She struggled to control it; if vandals came out, she would fight them.

The door opened a little more, then stopped, then a little more. She was puzzled. Had they seen her? She gritted her teeth and moved forward. Catch them by surprise. If they had guns, well, she was as good as dead anyway.

Then abruptly the door opened wider, and a dog stepped out. Kitty sat down on the ground in a sudden collapse of tension. After a moment she began to laugh, and for some time she couldn't stop. The dog came closer, wagging an absurd tail that was white-tipped and curled like a pig's. He was laughing too, or so it seemed to Kitty.

"What are you trying to do?" she said. "Scare a person to death? I thought you were armed robbers." She held out her hand, and he sniffed her fingers. "Where did you come from?" She tried to reach his collar, but that was a liberty he was not ready to grant. "Are you lost? Are you a runaway like me?" She tried to think of any of the cottagers who might have a dog like this—whatever this odd little dog was—but she knew of none. The Burgesses had a red setter, and the Migliorís had two Great Danes, and the Goulds had a Welsh terrier.

The dog sat down beside her, and they studied each other. Although she did not attempt to touch his collar again, she could not see that it had any name on it. "You couldn't be a stray. You look expensive. Well, there's nothing I can do about it, is there? And as long as you've already broken and entered, I'm going to see if there's anything to eat."

She felt uncomfortable going into the cottage, though she knew the Prentisses wouldn't mind. She stood a moment in the darkened living room, remembering playing with Timmy and his wooden train that was forever going off the track. He was a nice little boy. She went to the battered old upright piano the Prentisses had bought from the Methodist Church. Middle C was stuck and it was out of tune, but still it was a piano. "I wish," she said to the dog, "I could stay here and play and sing for a few hours." She laughed at his whimsical expression. "Hey, Sport, can you sing?"

In the kitchen she opened the cupboards. "Boy, they really shouldn't leave stuff like this." She took down three cans of tuna fish packed in water. "A good freeze and that stuff would bust all over the place." She found a battered frying pan under the sink, a can opener and an old spoon. To these she added a can of pink salmon, a jar of lemon marmalade, some deviled ham, a small can of baking powder, and a bag of flour partly used. She found a pencil and made a list in the margin of an old newspaper, noting the prices listed on the cans. "I'll have to guess at the flour." She printed a note. "DEAR MR. AND MRS. PRENTISS. I HAVE TAKEN SEVERAL THINGS THAT MIGHT HAVE SPOILED ANYWAYS. SEE LIST. HERE IS MONEY TO PAY AND A LITTLE OVER. YOU LEFT DOOR UNLOCKED. THANKS A LOT." She started to sign her name, then changed her mind. Anyone looking for her might pick up her trail. And the Prentisses might get into hot water for harboring a fugitive. She signed the note A FRIEND, and put the money with it.

She cleaned up the remaining pieces of kibble that the dog had scattered on the floor. "You're a litterer," she told him. "That's not nice."

With no apparent effort, he leaped up onto the kitchen table. She gasped. "Hey, get off there! What kind of manners have you got anyway?" She pushed him off. "But, boy, you can really jump. Like a fawn or something." She studied him. "You're a funny kind of dog."

Vaguely she remembered someone having said something like that—a dog that looked like a miniature deer. . . . "Coach," she said. "You must be the dog Coach saw. Listen, Sport, you better go home." She shooed him out and closed the back door as tightly as she could and found a piece of wood to wedge under it. "That'll keep it from blowing open anyway, keep out snow and varmints."

She picked up her kayak at the waterfront and made a pack out of her backpack, the kayak, and the paddle. "Not the most comfortable thing in the world, but it'll do," she said. "Now you go home, Sport, scat, get along." She tried to shoo him away, but he only danced a few feet off and came back. "I'm not playing games. I'm serious. I'm a fugitive, and I've got to make tracks right now before they come after me."

On the path, she put on her pack and balanced the kayak lengthwise on her back. The dog followed her, but she stopped and turned him toward the lake. "You're a real pretty dog and I like you, but I haven't got time to mess around with you now. Go home like a good dog. Go on." She stamped her foot.

He jumped sideways and ran up a pine tree as he had done with the little boys, peering down at her as if the next move in the game were hers. Like the boys, she stared at him in disbelief.

"That's not possible, what you did. Dogs can't do that." She stared at him, trying to figure out this strange miracle. Then the faint sound of a motorboat stirred her to action. "You may be magic, but I can't wait to see. So long, Sport, hope I see you again." She trotted up the path into the woods, the kayak thumping her back with every step.

As she got deeper into the woods, the going became harder. She had to walk bent forward to keep the top of the kayak from crashing into the branches. The little boat was a nuisance, but she would undoubtedly come to streams and lakes on her long trek, and the boat might make all the difference. And it would make a good shelter. As soon as she felt it was safe to stop, she would try to rearrange her burdens.

For nearly an hour she kept going without pause. At last she stopped beside a brook and lowered the kayak and the backpack to the thick pine needles.

It was cool in the woods, but she was perspiring from her hike. She threw herself down on her stomach and drank from the brook and ducked her head into the cold water. Then stretching out on her back, she closed her eyes.

She was almost asleep when she felt something cold and wet touch her cheek. She sat up in fright and then groaned. "Oh, no, not you." She flopped back, and the dog jumped lightly onto her chest and peered into her eyes. "I told you to stay. I told you and told you to go home. Why did you follow me? What am I going to do with you?"

He stretched out comfortably, his paws on her shoulders and his muzzle resting under her chin. She put her hands on the warm short coat and said, "Well, Sport, it looks as if I'm stuck with you for now. I can't remember how Aunt Lee feels about dogs. She got me a kitten, I remember that. If she says no to you, you'll have to go. If she lets you stay, you'll have to be very good and not eat more than I can afford to buy for you." It worried her about a job. What if she couldn't get one? She might have to go home and take the consequences. A vision of prison bars danced in front of her and she said, "No, I'll never go home." But she could not, no way, sponge on Aunt Lee.

"Well," she said to the dog, "here's lesson number one: worry about just one day at a time. You remind me if I forget."

CHAPTER SIX

THE dog was tired and so was Kitty. She decided to spend the night where they were, even though there were a number of hours of daylight left.

"I don't suppose it will make all that much difference if they're on my trail," she told the dog. "If they come after me with dogs or something, they'll find me anyway. Look how easy you found me. And I've got a blister on my heel." She searched through her pockets hoping to find a Band-Aid, but there were none. She folded a Kleenex in small squares and put it over the blister, inside her sock. "My shoes are too small. My shoes are always too small, because my feet go on getting bigger and bigger and bigger." She looked at his graceful paws. "Have you got your growth?"

He opened his mouth wide and gave a loud yawn.

She laughed. "You sound as if you're saying, 'Ohh, Gawd.' " She reached for the tag on his collar and read it, but it was only a rabies tag with a number. There was no name. "Your people might be looking for you. What I ought to do is, I ought to take you to some town and turn you in. The cops could trace you through your number."

He cocked his head on one side and looked at her intently, his forehead wrinkled.

"You look as if you're about to bust out crying. All right, I won't turn you in if you won't turn me in."

She offered him part of a can of tuna fish, but he sniffed and turned his head away. "So you're a picky eater. You could say thank you at least. What have I got you might deign to eat?" She looked at the salmon, the marmalade, the deviled ham, and the flour. "Nothing. If I'd known you'd be dropping in, I'd have brought something. You'll just have to go out in the woods and take pot luck. Are you a hunter?"

When she had finished the tuna fish, he came back and lapped the oil out of the can. Since she had time before dark, she decided to try making some bread. "I haven't done this since I was a Camp Fire Girl," she told the dog, who was watching every move she made. "Keep your fingers crossed." She gathered some dry twigs and broke off several dead branches from an old pine. "Now, we build our fire next to this boulder, see, so the heat will reflect. Got that?" She heaped up the twigs and broke the branches up, piling them loosely on the twigs. "Now, before we go any further, we dig a little hole right here by the fire to put hot coals in. A neat little oven. Hey, no, don't *you* dig. You go at it too hard." She pushed him away and brushed the loose dirt from his nose. "Games later, all right? Food first." She found a match and lit the fire, shielding the flame with her hands until it caught. "First match. Give me A for woodsmanship."

While the fire blazed up, she measured out what seemed to be about a cup of flour and a teaspoonful of baking powder. "No salt, sorry. It gives you cancer or something anyway. No, I guess it's high blood pressure. Aunt Lee can't eat much salt." She mixed the flour and baking powder, and then got some water in the drinking cup she carried in her pack. "Add enough water to make a good dough, see, Sport? Just like Julia Child. Me, I make a hole in the middle, to make it crustier." She put the frying pan on the edge of the fire to warm, and dusted the dough with flour. "It'll stick like crazy, without any shortening. You get to eat the burned pieces off the bottom." When the dough was ready, she put it into the frying pan and held it over the fire, rotating it gently. With her foot she knocked a few coals into the hole she had dug, and put the frying pan on top of them, to cook both from the heat of the coals and the heat from the flames.

She brushed the flour from her hand. "There. Now we wait."

The dog ventured too close to the hot coals and retreated with a little yowl.

"Fire burns, old boy. One of the facts of life." She stroked his nose. "I'm glad you came along. You're good company." She stretched out comfortably near the fire with her head on her knapsack. "Fire feels good, even on a warm day like this." The dog curled up beside her and put his muzzle on her knee. They dozed.

After a while the smell of the baking bread roused Kitty. She sat up, grabbed the handle of the frying pan, and gave it a flip that turned the bread over. "How's that? I could get a job in a pancake house. Some of it stuck to the bottom, but that's all right." She wandered a little way from the fire and found some highbush cranberries. She ate a handful. "Umm. Try it, you'll like it." But the dog sniffed and refused. She picked some more and came back to the fire to test the bread.

"Done to a turn." As soon as it had cooled enough to touch, she broke off a piece and offered it to the dog. This time, after some careful exploring of her hand, he ate it. "See? What'd I tell you?" She gave him some more and ate the rest herself. "Some butter would go good, but you can't have everything when you're pioneers like you and me." She let him nibble the charred pieces that stuck to the pan, and then with a handful of sand from the brook, she scrubbed the pan and rinsed it.

For the night she braced one end of the kayak against a tree at an angle and piled up some pine boughs at the foot. Now if it rained, they would have some shelter at least. She put her sweater back on, the sweater Aunt Lee had made for her last Christmas, too short in the sleeves, too tight across the shoulders, but a pretty, warm woolen sweater just the same. "Aunt

Lee wouldn't believe it if I told her my measurements now. Nobody would believe it. They make me sound like the Manhattan Mauler." She sighed. If somebody came along and offered her three wishes, she would wish first that Mort wasn't stretched out on some slab in a morgue; second, that she could be small and dainty and five foot two; and third, that Aunt Lee would be there and glad to see her.

During the night she woke once to find that the dog was not there. Toward dawn she was awakened again by a strange sound some distance away. It was an animal sound, but not one she had ever heard: a low mournful cry that rose in volume and pitch until it broke off in a high wail. It made her shiver. Animals she knew about, she could cope with; but what if those stories about Bigfoot were true? She found herself unable to go back to sleep, and she was relieved when the dog came back.

CHAPTER SEVEN

SHE tried not to think about food. They were down to the lemon marmalade and the remains of the flour and baking powder. Every now and then she stuck her finger into the marmalade jar and scooped out a bite. "Quick energy," she told the dog, but her energy did not feel quick at all. She was bone weary. It was their third day in the woods, and it had begun to rain. Without the sun for a guide, she was not even sure she was going in the right direction.

Toward evening they stopped in a clump of dense young pines that were low enough for her to balance the kayak on top of them like a roof.

The dog, whom she had decided to call Lucky, rubbed against her leg and then shook himself, showering her with raindrops. He was shivering.

She held out a finger and let him lick off some marmalade. "When you get home, you can tell 'em you've developed a whole bunch of new tastes. Lemon marmalade for supper, please." She put her arm around him. "I know. You're cold and hungry and slightly scared. Me too." She looked up and caught a raindrop in her eye. "Well, no good just standing here. Let's see if we can find some semi-dry wood for a fire." She was worried about her matches; there were only five left.

When she had the fire going, she felt somewhat cheered. If only they had some food. She didn't like to use the last of the flour yet. "Let's go look for berries," she said. It was still light enough to see.

During the day they had come across some dried-up blackberries and she had eaten them. But now she couldn't find anything that she was familiar enough with to eat, except a handful of wet clover that she chewed on without enthusiasm. "It'll never replace steak," she said.

Suddenly Lucky took off, streaking up a slope in long leaps. A startled grouse whirred up out of the undergrowth just ahead of him, ran a few steps, and then flew along about a foot above the ground, flapping his short wings in a desperate effort to stay ahead of Lucky. But the dog easily ran circles around the bird, startling it out of its path.

Kitty watched, holding her breath. Roast grouse for supper? Her mouth began to water. But in spite of her hunger, she found herself hoping the grouse would get away.

Lucky sprang up on a granite rock and off again directly in the path of the panicked bird. The grouse flew higher, and the dog leaped up, his head actually brushing the feet of the grouse. But he made no effort to kill it or even to knock it down. He forced the grouse to circle, and it flew back toward Kitty and past her head so close she could feel the scattered raindrops from its wings. And then it was gone, and Lucky was sitting at her feet, panting, his mouth wide and his tongue out.

"You must be some kind of retriever," she said. "You don't kill. Well, I haven't got a gun, old sport. No grouse for supper." She went back to the warmth of the fire, the dog trotting quietly behind her, as if he had done his part and was ready to rest. He lay down close to the fire and put his head on his paws.

An overhang of rocks protected the fire from the steady rain, and to some extent the trees and the kayak protected Kitty. Lucky curled up in her lap, his white-tipped tail wound tight as a spring, and as the cold gray afternoon merged into colder night, they dozed.

Hours later Lucky woke her by jumping off her lap. The fire had gone out, and the night seemed thick and black. She couldn't tell whether the water dripping steadily all around her was rain or moisture from the trees.

"Lucky?" She couldn't see him or hear him. Stiffly she rebuilt the fire and used one more precious match to get it going. As the kindling caught, she looked up at a sound near her, thinking it was Lucky. "Where'd you go. . . ?" She stopped short, catching her breath. A large bear stood framed between two trees looking at her with lowered head. She was scared. She had never come across a bear before, and this one did not look friendly. Then the fire flared up, the bear shook his head, turned, and disappeared.

She began to worry about Lucky. But though she called and whistled, it was another half hour before he came back. He jumped into her lap, soaking wet and shivering. She held him close, and soon the heat of the new fire made the night more comfortable for them both.

When a sullen gray light in the east just slightly changed the look of the sky, she stood up and tried to fix the direction in her mind. "The game trail we were on when you flushed the partridge," she said, "must go east. At least for a while. Let's put out the fire and get going while we still have a clue."

It was hard to leave the warmth of the fire and trudge along the sodden path, hungry, wet, and cold. She found herself thinking about bacon and eggs, pancakes, hot coffee, johnny cake, Aunt Lee's blueberry muffins, fried ham. She was going to have to find a place soon where she could buy food. Going into a town was very scary. There might be an APB out on her, and local cops would spot her right away. She'd probably be the tallest Wanted Female in New England. Maybe her picture was already up in the local post offices. But she would have to do something or she would starve.

The top of the kayak caught on a branch and nearly threw her to the ground. When she pulled, the frame wouldn't give. "Darn it!" She gave an impatient jerk, and as the boat came loose, the wet canvas caught her in the face.

Maybe it was stupid to tug the thing along. But it had sheltered them the night before, and if they came to a lake or a wide river, it would be useful. She decided to keep it a while longer.

Lucky darted into the brush again and after some commotion came back with a field mouse. He sat down in front of Kitty with a satisfied air and ate it.

"Yuk," Kitty said. "I'm not that hungry yet." But she was beginning to feel weak from lack of food. Soon she would make some bread with the last of the flour. It was no treat, but it might keep up her strength a little longer.

The sky stayed gray and dense, but the rain stopped. All day they followed the trail that Lucky had found, and in the afternoon it broadened into a rough road, with faint Jeep tracks. The tracks worried her. What if a cop or a ranger was out looking for her? She wished she knew exactly where she was. The walking, at least, was easier now, without the constant obstruction of trees. "Maybe we'll get somewhere yet," she told Lucky.

She could tell that the dog was tired. Often he stopped and sat down as if he were not going to walk another step. When he stopped, she waited, letting him rest, but in a few minutes she would coax him on. Finally he flopped down on his stomach at her feet and looked up at her, his tongue lolling from his mouth. She gave him some water from the canteen, splashing it into the frying pan so he could drink. The water was nearly gone, but so far water had not been a problem.

She sat down on a log and drank a little herself, but it gave her a cramp in her empty stomach. She put a pine needle in her mouth and chewed on it, enjoying the sharp flavor. "I'll never go off in the woods again," she said, "without getting me one of those books about recognizing wild foods. I'm hungry enough to eat skunk cabbage."

When she was ready to go, Lucky didn't move. She coaxed him, and then walked along a way, expecting him to follow, but he just whimpered a little and stayed where he was. She sighed. "All right." She went back and lifted him into her backpack. He sat quietly while she heaved the pack onto her back and adjusted the shoulder straps. "I'm glad you're not a St. Bernard," she told him. "And I guess it's a good thing I didn't get my wish about being little and delicate. Hang on, here we go." She carried the kayak under her arm.

He rode with his chin on her shoulder. She was so tired, the extra weight hardly seemed to make much difference. Her shoulders and back ached, but they had been aching for a long time. Doggedly, she bent forward and put one foot down after another, counting aloud to keep a rhythm. Then she decided to sing to cheer herself up. She sang everything she could think of that could be made into a marching song.

She had just finished "When the Caissons Go Rolling Along," when a crash in the trees ahead of her brought her to a stop. A white-tailed deer broke out of the brush and leaped across the road, disappearing again on the other side. Lucky struggled to get out of the backpack.

"Hold still," she said. "It was only a deer." But he managed to squirm out of the pack and leaped to the ground, bounding off after the deer. She called him, but he paid no attention. In a smaller version of the deer's graceful bounds, Lucky sailed across the deadwood piled by the road and disappeared. At the instant he was gone, Kitty felt a stirring of air past her head, and immediately afterward heard the report of a gun. She yelled and dived for the ground, jerking the kayak over her head.

A man came out of the woods, his gun ready. Kitty peered cautiously from under the kayak. "Hey!" she shouted. "Watch it!"

He seemed not to hear her, but after a moment he saw her, and his mouth fell open. "What the heck . . . !"

She got up. "Listen, you'd better watch it. You darn near hit me. You could kill somebody." She was shaking with shock and anger.

"I didn't hit you, did I?" His voice was unnaturally loud, and it occurred to her that he was deaf.

"No, but you almost did. My dog is out there. You be good and darned careful. . . ."

"Did you see a deer? I got a shot in, but I don't think I hit him. Which way'd he go?"

Kitty put her hands on her hips and yelled. "You watch out for my dog!"

"I'm sorry." He pointed to his ears. "Got ear plugs in. Can't hear you. Which way'd he go, did you say?"

Kitty advanced toward him. She was considerably bigger than he was, and he backed away. "Take out your ear plugs." She gestured toward his ears.

Startled by her size and her fierce look, he hurried off into the brush, at an angle from the direction the deer and Lucky had taken. Just before he disappeared, he looked back and called, "Listen, you ought not to be in the woods without you wear something orange. You could get hit." And he was gone.

Kitty sat down on the ground, her knees weak. At least he had gone in the wrong direction, but the deer might have circled. If she called Lucky, she might lead him right into the hunter's path. If she didn't call him . . . She felt like crying.

"Hel-*lo,*" a surprised voice said behind her. "What in the world are you doing here?"

She turned and saw a tall young man in an orange vest, a peaked cap on his head that said PENZOIL, and a shotgun in his hand. "Are you all right?" Then more anxiously, "My brother didn't hit you, did he? My God! Are you hit?"

"No." She got up. "But no thanks to that guy, your brother or whoever. Is he insane or what?"

He looked relieved. "No, just . . . uh . . . impulsive."

"Well, a gun is no toy for somebody that impulsive. He nearly hit me. And if he hits my dog, I'll kill him."

"Oh, he won't hit your dog."

"He nearly hit *me.*"

"Yes, but you're more the size of . . ." He stopped, realizing what he had been about to say. "A person is closer to the size of a doe. A dog—what kind of dog is it?"

"I don't know. Just a dog."

"I mean how big?"

She showed him with her hands.

"Oh, Byron won't hit a dog."

"I'm glad you're so confident." She brushed the dust off her jeans.

"You ought to be wearing orange, though," he said politely. He came closer. "What is that? It looks like a kayak."

"It's what it looks like." She knew she was being rude to the wrong person, but she was still too shaken up to be friendly.

"I see. I thought it was." He looked at her sideways.

"I don't approve of hunters," she said severely.

"Oh. Well, you don't need to worry about me. I never hit anything in my life. I just come along to keep Byron out of trouble."

"You'd be better off to take him bowling."

He looked at her a second and then burst out laughing. He laughed with such genuine enjoyment that finally she had to laugh too. "Listen," he said, "what makes you think *that* would be safe? Byron would be sure to hit somebody with the bowling ball."

"But it wouldn't be my dog."

He grew serious. "You're really worried about your dog, aren't you."

"Of course, I'm worried."

"Have you called him?" Before she could stop him, he whistled, loud and long. "That'll either bring Byron or the dog."

"Nobody should put earstoppers in their ears when they go hunting. That's insane."

"The bang hurts his ears." He helped her strap on her backpack. "Where are you heading?"

"East," she said shortly.

"I see."

After a moment of indecision she said, "Uh, am I heading in the right direction? Does this road go east?"

He pulled back his sleeve and looked at a compass strapped to his wrist like a watch. "Almost due east, but a little bit north. I'm not sure if this road runs east all the way though. You weren't lost, were you?"

"Oh, not really. I just wasn't sure."

"Look," he said, unstrapping the compass. "Take this." When she started to refuse, he said, "No, really, take it. I got it for Christmas when I was a Boy Scout, that's how old it is. Byron has a fancy one from L. L. Bean, so I don't need this." He held it out to her.

"Are you sure?"

"Sure I'm sure."

She took it gratefully. "Do you know if there's a town near here?"

He thought a minute. "The nearest one I know is Peddler's Fork. It's just a dinky little place with a bar and one store and a little diner. About a mile down this road, and then take a trail that strikes off to your right; it'll be about a mile and a half down that trail. You'll come to a county road, and there you are."

"Good." She tried to sound casual. "I'm running low on grub."

"Oh." He pulled a stick of jerky from his pocket and gave it to her. "Tide you over."

"Thanks." It took self-control not to stuff it into her mouth immediately, but she made herself unwrap it slowly.

"I'd better go find Byron. Which way did he go?"

She pointed it out.

"If I see your dog, I'll tell him . . ." He stopped as Lucky leaped out of the woods and ran to Kitty, jumping up for her to catch him in her arms.

"Oh, Lucky! I'm so glad to see you!" Her eyes filled with tears. "I thought you'd get killed." She hugged him hard, and he gave her a quick kiss on the cheek.

"He's beautiful," the young hunter said. "He's a basenji, isn't he?"

She looked at him blankly for a moment. She had forgotten he was there. "Oh," she said. "Yeah."

He held out his hand, and Lucky sniffed it carefully. "You're a beauty. No wonder your lady didn't want you to get hurt." He pulled a length of white nylon rope from his own small backpack and cut off a long piece. "You could use this for a leash till you get him out of the range of Byron. So he won't run off again."

She was pleased. "Can you spare it?"

"Sure. It's to pack out the deer Byron gets, but he won't get one. By the time Byron comes crashing through the trees, any deer with a lick of sense is five miles away." He coiled a loop of rope and attached it to Lucky's collar. "There you are." He stood looking down at the dog a moment. "He's used to a leash, you can tell." He handed the end of the rope to Kitty. "Well, I got to go. Where are you from? Maybe I'll see you again sometime."

She answered him without thinking, and then realized she shouldn't have told him.

But he just said, "Is that in Maine?"

"Uh, no," she said. "It's in Vermont actually. I'm visiting relatives." She shifted the kayak. "Well, thanks again. Watch out for your brother."

"Right."

At the top of a slight hill she turned and saw him standing there and waved. He waved back and then moved off into the woods.

"He was really nice," she said to Lucky. "But that brother ought to be locked up." Lucky turned his inquisitive face toward her. "And you, running off like a . . . like some kind of deer. You mustn't do that. You scared me to death. What did he call you? A basengy, basenji . . . something? I never heard of it. No wonder you're different. Well, friend, we're heading for Peddler's Fork and twenty-five hamburgers. How do you like yours?" She leaned down to pat his head and nearly lost her balance, which made her laugh. All at once she felt jubilant. Not afraid, not scared. She sang "Home on the Range" loud and clear, as they marched along the road to Peddler's Fork, sharing the stick of jerky.

CHAPTER EIGHT

"WHAT am I going to do with you?" Kitty said to Lucky. "If I take you into town, everybody'll notice us. I have a hard enough time being inconspicuous, without taking along a weird-type dog." She shaded her eyes. "The town's right down the road. I can see roofs. Listen, I'll have to tie you up till I get some food for us, but I won't be long, so don't panic, all right?" She led him off the road, tied him to a pine tree, and put her pack and the kayak under the tree. "Watch these for me. And don't get your rope tangled up. Stay, Lucky." She pointed her finger at him as he strained to follow her. "Lucky, stay."

Before she was over the crest of the hill, she heard him howl. It was not like a dog howl, more like an almost human being in terrible distress. If he kept that up, everybody within earshot would be coming out to see what in the world that noise was.

She passed a few scattered houses set back from the road, poor looking places with chickens scratching in front and small children playing in the dirt. They looked like houses in her own town. She waved to a couple of children, and they stared back at her, thumbs in mouth.

There was a gas station and then the little store that Byron's brother had mentioned. A man in a straw hat sat on the steps drinking a Pepsi, watching her as she came down the street. She nodded, and he returned the nod. A little further on she came to the diner. A middle-aged woman, small and anxious-looking, stood on the steps, her hands folded under her apron. When Kitty came toward her, she said, "Afternoon," and held open the door. There was no one else inside.

"Can I get some hamburgers, please?" Kitty said.

"Sure can." The woman gave her a tired smile. "How many?"

Kitty glanced at the bill of fare posted on the wall. Hamburgers were fifty cents. "Ten, please."

The woman's eyes widened. "Ten? Okay. It may take a few minutes. My assistant just quit on me. Right before suppertime. Wouldn't you know? You want them burgers plain or with?"

"With, please." She felt nervous. She couldn't hear Lucky, but he was probably still yowling. "I'll be back in a few minutes," she said. "I have to buy some things at the store."

The woman nodded and went into the tiny kitchen.

The man on the steps of the store got up and followed her in. "What can I do for you?"

"Do you have dog food?"

"Sure do." He pointed to some huge sacks of dog food.

"Oh. Anything smaller?"

He grinned. "I thought a girl as big as you could handle a big one."

She tried to smile. That kind of remark she never quite got used to, but she knew people meant no harm by it. "Maybe if you have a two- or three-pound bag . . . Oh, that one's fine." She looked around the store. "Have you got any cheese?"

"Sure. Cheddar, Swiss, pimiento, Cheese-whiz, Monterey jack . . ."

She picked out two packages of cheddar, a jar of peanut butter, a loaf of bread, and some apples.

"Just passin' through town?" he said, as he rang up her money.

"Yes."

He looked past her. "Don't see a car. You one of them backpackers?"

He made her nervous. "Oh, I and my friends are just taking a hike," she said.

"Where you from?"

She pretended not to hear him as she gathered up her change and her bag of groceries, but he asked her again. "A little town up the line a way," she said. "Nobody ever heard of it." She left quickly before he could think of more questions. Just like home, people wanting to know all about your business. But he seemed just nosey, rather than suspicious.

She listened for a moment but could not hear Lucky. In the diner the woman was still frying the hamburgers and slicing the onions. The radio was on, someone singing "Bryan's Song." She sat at the counter reading the menu over and over, humming the song. The frying beef smelled wonderful, and it was hard to sit there without eating something. She took an apple out of the bag.

"Want a cup of coffee while you wait?" the woman said.

"Thank you."

The woman pushed back the half-dollar Kitty put down on the counter. "Anybody buys ten hamburgers gets a cup of coffee on the house." She pushed her hair back from her forehead. "I'll have a cup with you. I'm beat." She glanced at the clock. "Supper trade'll be along soon. That darned Muriel. She could at least have given me notice so's I could get somebody else." She gave Kitty an appraising glance. "Wouldn't want a job for a few days, would you?"

Kitty hesitated. She would like to help this nice woman out, but what would she do with Lucky? And what if somebody recognized her from an APB or something? It was a tiny place, hardly a village, but there must be cops that came through, and cops always ate at diners. "I have a dog with me," she said. "I couldn't bring him into town. He howls, and he'd probably run away."

"You could leave him at my house." The woman

looked pleading. "You could bunk there. I'm alone now."

"He might do a lot of damage."

"We can leave him in the kitchen. I don't live close to neighbors, so it wouldn't matter if he howled."

Kitty was scared, but she couldn't think of any way to refuse without seeming unkind. "Well, maybe for a day or two."

"Oh, bless you." Quickly the woman drew a map on the back of a menu. "Door's unlocked. Just leave the dog in the kitchen and be back here by six, all right?" As Kitty still looked hesitant, she said, "Look, I'll pay top price. More than top. Five dollars an hour."

"It isn't that. We were on our way somewhere. I couldn't stay long."

"Even a couple of days would be a godsend. I'll put an ad in the paper, but it only comes out once a week." She put her hand against her chest. "I got this silly blood pressure. Doc says take it easy, but that's easier said than done."

"I'll be here at six," Kitty said. You couldn't be mean to a nice lady with high blood pressure. But two days would be it. Beyond that she'd be pushing her luck too far. Somebody would recognize her, or recognize Lucky, and if they got on the trail of the dog, they'd be on her trail, too. She'd probably get jumped for dognapping, and then they'd find out she had a murder rap she was running away from. It was kind of like TV, and if it hadn't been so threatening, it would have been exciting. But Kitty was frightened.

"You don't know how much I appreciate it. Listen, you still want all those hamburgers?"

"Yes, please."

When the woman had them cooked and had added onion and pickles and ketchup, Kitty paid her and said, "I'll be back by six."

This time there were three men on the steps of the grocery store, drinking beer. The proprietor of the store called out to her as if she were an old friend. "Watch your step, Lanky."

She waved and walked faster. As soon as she was past the gas station, she heard Lucky. She broke into a run.

"Darn you, Lucky!" He had almost chewed through the rope, and he had scattered her belongings all around the tree. "Why do you have to be so bad? Look, I've got food, lots of it." She gave him a hamburger—pickle, onion, and all—and he ate it in a couple of gulps. "Don't be greedy." She opened two more and shared them with him. "I've got a job for a couple of days. You're going to have to be good, though."

When all ten hamburgers were gone, she stretched out on her stomach for a few minutes, Lucky settled comfortably in the small of her back. Then reluctantly she turned over and got up. "Got work to do." She assembled her gear, put the groceries in her pack, decided to hoist the kayak onto the lower branches of a big willow, and started down the road toward town. At the narrow dirt road marked on the map, she turned off, and in a minute she came to a small frame house set alone in a clearing. It was a neat-looking place, with the last of a flower garden leaning against a picket fence.

"It feels funny to go into a stranger's house, but she said to," Kitty said to Lucky. She pushed open the front door and the dog bounded in ahead of her and leaped up onto a leather couch.

"Get off the furniture. Where are your manners?" She put her things in the tiny bedroom off the kitchen. "I've got time for a quick shower. What luxury!"

Lucky kept thrusting his nose past the white shower curtain into the shower stall until water splashed into his face, and he withdrew with an offended look.

Kitty emerged with her shampooed hair slicked back, feeling as refreshed as if she'd had a long rest. She left Lucky in the kitchen with a pan of drinking water and a little of the dog food. "Though how you can eat one more bite, I don't know."

It was only twenty of six when she got to the diner and found her new employer frying potatoes. "Here, let me do that," she said. "I used to work in a little café."

The woman sat down. "The good Lord must have been looking after me when He sent you to town. What's your name, dear?"

"Kitty."

The woman didn't press her for a last name. "I'm

Myrtle Backus." She nodded toward the small sign that said 'Myrt's Place.' She poured herself a cup of decaffeinated coffee and added artificial cream from a paper envelope. "My husband and I took this place ten years ago, but he died back here in 1978, right after Christmas."

"I'm sorry he died," Kitty said.

Mrs. Backus sighed. "Yes. I miss him."

"Do you have children?"

"One girl, but she lives in the state of Washington. I haven't seen her for three years." She took a billfold from a shelf under the counter and held it, opened, toward Kitty. "Those are my grandkids. That's Laurie on the left, and the one in the cowboy hat is Jeff."

Kitty examined the picture and said, "They look like terrific kids."

"Remind me when we get home to show you the letters Laurie writes me. They're a riot." She got up and smoothed out her apron.

"I hope my dog won't do any damage," Kitty said. "I left him in the kitchen." She shook the fat from the wire basket the potatoes were in and set them in the warmer.

"Nothing he can hurt in the kitchen. What kind of dog is it?"

"It's called a basenji."

"Don't know them. I'm a cat person myself, but my old tom passed away this summer, and I haven't got me a new cat yet." She looked out the window as a truck drove up. "Here we go. The rush is on."

The customers never amounted to a rush, but there were enough of them for the next two hours to keep Kitty and Mrs. Backus busy. Toward the end the man who ran the grocery store came in with another man and ordered coffee. He grinned when he saw Kitty.

"Well, hi there, Highpockets. Didn't know you was working for Myrt."

Kitty flushed, and Mrs. Backus answered for her. "That's not a very nice way to speak to a girl, Horace Smiley. How would you like it if we was to call you Fatso?" She glanced significantly at his pot belly.

"Wouldn't care for it." He gave Kitty a little bow, half ironic, half genuinely apologetic. "Sorry 'bout that."

"That's okay," she said, but she was glad Mrs. Backus had put him down. She was sure he meant no harm, but he was too much like some of her father's friends.

When everyone but Horace Smiley and his friend Joe had gone, Mrs. Backus piled two plates with food for Kitty and herself, turned the CLOSED sign around on the door, and sat down in one of the four booths.

When they had nearly finished their dinner, the music on the radio stopped and the announcer gave the station's call letters. "And now here is the Dog-Gone Show, for pets lost and found, and any other lost and found articles." He read several bulletins about missing cats, a missing Collie, a found parakeet, a lost wallet. And then he said, "Here's a missing dog, reward offered by the kennel the dog disappeared from. Male basenji"—he stumbled over the word—"reddish brown, white markings on face and chest and feet, curled tail, answers to name of Haile, that's H-a-i-l-e, as in Haile Selassie. Reward. Call this station if you have seen this dog. And that's all tonight for the Dog-Gone Show. This is your Rochester station for news, sports, and easy listening."

Kitty gave her entire attention to the piece of apple pie she was eating.

"Reward," Horace Smiley said. "I'd like to find me that dog."

"You couldn't find anything if it was right under your nose," Mrs. Backus said sharply. When Kitty looked up, she met her eyes for a second and then looked away.

"What you taking out after me for tonight, Myrt?" Horace said. "You feeling poorly?"

"I feel fine." Mrs. Backus got up. "Don't mind me, Horace. But we got to close up now. You boys finish off that cold coffee you been nursing along hoping I'd give you refills. You know the price of coffee?"

Kitty was silent while they finished washing up. On the way home Mrs. Backus chatted about the town and the people in it, but made no reference to the radio item. When they came near the house, Lucky's keening howl reached them.

"Goodness," Mrs. Backus said, "got a funny howl, hasn't he?"

"Yes," Kitty said. Lucky leaped up almost to her shoulders when they came into the kitchen.

"He likes you," Mrs. Backus said.

Holding the dog in her arms Kitty looked directly at Mrs. Backus. "I guess you're thinking I must have swiped him."

"No such thing."

"Well, I didn't. He was in the woods near my house—well, not near exactly, but down at the end of the lake. I told him and told him to go home, but he didn't. I thought he had, because he disappeared, but he'd been following me, I guess, and later he caught up with me. I didn't even know what kind of dog he was till I met a man in the woods near here, a man out hunting, and he said it was a basenji. I never heard of them." Her eyes filled with tears. "But I like him a lot."

"And he likes you. So why don't the two of you just get on to bed and get some sleep. I open up for lunch at 11:30, so sleep as late as you want."

Kitty glanced at the phone on the wall. "They'll take him away from me."

"Who will?"

"If anyone sees him, they'll call up the station."

"Who's going to see him? Just be sure you latch the kitchen door when you go out."

"There's a reward."

"Do you want it?"

Kitty looked shocked. "Oh, no!"

"Then quit worrying. *I'm* not going to turn him in, if that's what's worrying you. I'm not so hard up for cash I'd turn in a girl's dog, just to send him back to some old kennel."

"You're awfully good."

"Get along with you." The woman aimed a light slap at Kitty's arm. She looked pleased. "Want a glass of milk before you turn in?"

"Oh, gosh, no. I haven't eaten so much in my life as I've eaten today."

The woman filled a glass with water and reached for a small bottle of pills. "My trusty friends." She held up the bottle. "If there's one thing I wouldn't want, it's a stroke."

"Listen," Kitty said, "if you feel bad or anything, you call me."

The woman smiled. "Good night, Kitty. I hope you stay a long time."

CHAPTER NINE

WHEN she joined Myrt for breakfast in the kitchen, Kitty flopped down into a canvas chair, and it collapsed with a sickening rip of cloth and cracking of wood. She was overcome with embarrassment.

"Forget it," Myrt said. "I never did like that chair. No kind of chair to have in a kitchen. I got it with green stamps ages ago." She helped Kitty out of the debris.

"Oh, gosh, I'm so sorry. My father says I come into a room like a rampaging horse, and he's right. I break everything I touch."

"Don't worry about it. You're just not built on the same scale as most of us. Nowadays they skimp so on everything, stuff seems to be made for midgets like me."

"I should tell you," Kitty said, "the last time I worked in a cafe, I got fired by the boss's wife for breaking glasses."

Myrt laughed. "You'd have to break everything we've got before I'd fire a girl that works as hard and as willing as you."

"Don't be too sure I won't." But Myrt's acceptance of her clumsiness made her feel better. Here was one person who didn't treat her like some kind of objectionable freak.

After breakfast she made Myrt sit down with the morning paper, and she washed the dishes very carefully, fed and walked Lucky, and vacuumed the rugs.

"You spoil me so, I'm never going to let you go," Myrt said, when they finally closed the door on the disappointed Lucky and walked to the diner.

Lunchtime was busy. Local business people and a good many truck drivers stopped in, and they all knew Myrt. Some of them were curious about Kitty, and from the kitchen she could hear Myrt answering their questions with, "I didn't ask for her family tree. All I know is, she works good, and she's got a heart as big as all outdoors."

Right after the two o'clock news she heard the Dog-Gone Show coming on the air again and she paused, her hands in soapy dishwater. Only three or four customers were in the diner, but they all were local people. After the usual lost and found cats and dogs, the announcer said, "We still have that dog with the weird name. . . ." Kitty held her breath. But Myrt casually reached up and switched the radio to a different station, and Kitty breathed again.

Just as they were closing for the interval between lunch and dinner, Horace Smiley burst out of the door of his grocery store and ran toward them. He yelled excitedly.

"Seen that dog! The one they got a reward for."

Kitty gasped. "Where?"

He pointed down the street, and Kitty saw Lucky pursuing a gray cat.

Myrt pushed her. "Quick! Get him before Horace does."

Kitty leaped the diner's steps and ran down the road, easily passing the short-legged Horace. She heard him yell a protest, but she paid no attention.

"Lucky!" she called. "Lucky, come here!"

The dog abandoned the cat chase at once and bounded toward her, leaping into her arms. She looked for a way to avoid Horace, but he was almost up to her, with Myrt close behind him and breathing hard.

"Hey," Horace called, "I found that dog. You never woulda seen him. . . ."

Myrt caught up with them as Horace reached for Lucky. "Go home," she said to Kitty. "Hurry up."

"Look here, Myrt," Horace said. He was red with exertion and anger. "I lay claim to that dog."

"Possession is nine points, Horace," Myrt said, and as she walked more slowly after Kitty, she called back, "If we get a reward, we'll split it with you, Horace. Don't be greedy."

Kitty ran all the way to the house, carrying Lucky, who squirmed to be let down. She burst into the kitchen through the open door and didn't let go of him until she had the nylon rope securely attached to his collar.

"Darn you, how did you get out?" She was almost in tears. "You've gone and ruined everything. We'll have to leave, right when Mrs. Myrt needs us. How could you do such a stupid thing?"

Lucky sat down and looked at her, his forehead wrinkled and his dark eyes troubled.

"Oh, all right," she said more quietly. "I'm not really mad at you, but I just wish you had stayed where you were put."

In a few minutes Myrt came, out of breath. "Whew!" She sank into the rocker by the window. "Haven't walked that fast in a couple years. You little scamp, how'd you get that door open?"

"He's like a cat. He can do anything." Kitty looked at Myrt with a worried frown. "I'll either have to leave now or give him up."

Myr nodded sadly. "I know. Horace is bound to be on the phone right now. You'll have to go right away." She sighed. "I knew you were too good to be true."

"Listen," Kitty said, "I don't want to leave you without any help. Maybe if we hid him . . ."

Myrt shook her head. "You know he wouldn't stay hid. No, I'll be all right. I was thinking last night, if you should leave—and I knew you would sooner or later—maybe I could put an announcement on that radio station for a girl to help me. There must be girls would like the job, if I could reach them. "I've used the paper before but I didn't think of radio."

Relieved, Kitty said, "That's a neat idea. Will you do it right away? Call them up right away, okay?"

"I will, but we'd better get you on your way." She got up and began taking things from the cupboard. "You won't have time to buy anything so you just pack a few things in your backpack. . . ." She sorted out some cans of sardines, some dried milk, apricots, baked beans, coffee. "You get your things together, honey. You want to get as good a start as you can. I'll go back and stall Horace somehow. Which way are you heading?" She turned and looked at Kitty. "I don't even know your last name."

Kitty had brought her pack into the kitchen and was stowing away the food. "My name is Kitty LeBlanc," she said in a low voice. "I'm running away because I knocked a man down that was pestering me, and I think he might be dead."

Myrt looked up sharply. "You think? You don't know?"

"I didn't wait to find out."

"Child," Myrt said, "if anybody had been killed in these parts, it would have been all over the radio."

For the first time Kitty felt a stab of hope. "You haven't heard anything?"

"Nothing. Why don't you just go on back home? Even if it turned out bad, if some man was bothering you and you hit him in self defense . . ."

She shook her head. "Nobody'd believe me. Except maybe a few friends."

"Why not?"

"Well, my father has a bad reputation. He's drunk a lot, and he gets in fights. People would say, 'Chip off the old block.' "

"What about your mother?"

"She's dead. I'm going to her friend in Maine. She'll take me in."

Myrt opened her mouth to answer, but Lucky suddenly ran to the door, cocked his head, and stared toward the path.

"He hears someone," Kitty said.

CHAPTER TEN

HORACE," Myrt said. "Quick, go down cellar and out through the bulkhead. Follow the path through the woods. You'll be heading east. God bless you." She reached up, gave Kitty a quick kiss, and headed her toward the cellar door. On the way she thrust something small into Kitty's pocket.

Kitty tugged on Lucky's rope, and with the pack under her other arm, she raced down the cellar stairs, pushed up the bulkhead doors, and ran down the path to the wood.

She didn't stop running until she was brought up short by a lightning-struck tree that had blocked the path. Lucky sailed over it with ease, but she had to drop her pack on the other side and then climb over. I could probably jump it myself, she thought, but sure as the world, I'd trip and fall on my stupid face.

On the other side she stood still listening, but the only sounds were the muted voices of the birds, sounding sleepy in the noonday warmth, and a couple of chipmunks who were chasing each other from one tree to another, chirruping like mechanical toys. She set out again at a steady pace, secure in the knowledge that she could outdistance fat old Horace any time. The thing was, though, if he called the kennel that owned Lucky, they might be better at catching up with her.

"I'd be willing to bet," she said to Lucky, "Myrt will give them a false steer. That Myrt, she's some kind of lady, isn't she? I don't feel good about leaving her, not good at all. I hope she finds somebody right away."

They moved along on the well-marked path until about five in the afternoon. It was getting dark and clouds were rolling up in the west. She wished she hadn't had to leave the kayak; it looked as if they were in for some rain.

"We'd better hole up here," she told Lucky. She had taken him off the rope, but he had not ventured far from her. She wondered if he sensed the danger. Dogs could probably tell when people were scared.

She found a mossy place just off the path, and by pulling down branches and weaving them together, she was able to make a fairly tight shelter though she knew it wouldn't keep them dry if a heavy rain began.

"At least we've got plenty of food." She gave him some of the dog food and opened a can of beans for herself. There was fresh running water in a brook nearby. She longed to build a fire, but she was afraid if anyone were pursuing her, they would see the smoke. After dark, perhaps she could risk a small one for warmth and comfort. The dark woods were not her favorite place to spend the night, though what she was afraid of, she could not have said.

"Do dogs inherit fears?" she asked Lucky. He looked up at her with his mouth full of the dog food, then swallowed it in one gulp. "No, you aren't afraid of much, I guess. You can outrun anything. But remember, it's not smart not to be scared *some*times. If you hadn't been so brave and bold and smart, we wouldn't be out here in the woods." She thought with longing of the comfortable bed in Myrt's guestroom. It had been too short for her, of course, but she had long since grown accustomed to sleeping with her feet hanging over the edge of whatever bed she was on.

She huddled up against the rough bark of the white pine and tried to think. Myrt said the path she was on went east, and the compass told her that that was nearly right; actually a little bit north of east. If she had only picked up a map at the gas station while she had the chance. She was carrying in her head the location of Aunt Lee's town, and she could be off some, but anyway once she got to Maine and the coast, she would be all right. The southern neck of Maine that she was approaching was narrow. She ought to come out somewhere close to Ogunquit, and then Aunt Lee's village was only a few miles up the coast.

If only Aunt Lee didn't mind her coming . . . that was the thing that worried around in the back of her mind. She tried not to think about it. One day at a time was enough to worry about. But when she was tired and sat thinking, the picture came to her of herself trudging up to Aunt Lee's door, and Aunt Lee looking at her with dismay and saying, "Whatever am I going to do with you?" Of worse yet, Aunt Lee not there at all. What if she had moved? What if she had . . . what if she had died?

Kitty got up abruptly, bumping her head and dislodging part of her carefully constructed roof. It was then she realized that Lucky wasn't with her.

She fought down a panicky urge to call him. If anybody had followed her through the woods, no sense in letting him know where she was or that Lucky was running around loose. She drank a lot of cold water from the brook, one of her long-time remedies for anxiety, but this time it didn't help much. She walked a little way from her campsite, but it was too dark now to see anything.

About an hour later, as she sat half dozing with her back to the tree, Lucky returned. He landed in her lap with a thud, circled two or three times, and settled down to sleep. The rain never came, but there was such a strong wind that Kitty didn't dare start a fire.

In the morning she was tired and stiff and hungry, and again she ate a cold meal. She felt depressed. Leaving nice Mrs. Myrt in the lurch was not a good thing to have done. She poured some milk into her old frying pan and gave it to Lucky.

"For such a tidy dog," she said, "you make a lot of noise when you drink."

She put her hand in her pocket for a Kleenex and

brought out some paper. Folded into a small packet were three ten-dollar bills. Myrt must have put them there.

"She gave me too much," Kitty said. "I'd have had to work a week at home to get that much. Listen, Lucky, when we get to Aunt Lee's, we're going to send Mrs. Myrt a real nice present. Don't forget."

She felt cheered, not so much by the money as by the kindness of a woman who scarcely knew her. People could be really great sometimes. She thought of Joe and of Coach and of Mick's father who let her use his boathouse, and the Prentisses. And now Mrs. Myrt.

At a fork in the path, she stopped and consulted her compass. The trail to the left was less well-traveled, but it seemed to be the one she wanted.

The wind died down, and the day grew warm. At noon she stopped on the bank of a river. "Now is when we could use the kayak," she said. "How deep do you suppose that is?"

In answer, Lucky plunged in and swam to the other side, where he stood shaking himself and looking at her as if impatient for her to follow him.

"Here goes nothing." She held her pack over her head and waded in cautiously, feeling the way for unexpected drops in the stream bottom. Once she stumbled and nearly fell, but she caught herself and kept going. The deepest part of the river, at the middle of the current, came barely to her hips.

She waded ashore and squeezed as much water out

of her jeans as she could. "One time it was good I'm tall."

Lucky sprinted around her in a wide circle, running as fast as he could go.

"That's the idea," she said. "Exercise. It'll help dry me out." She ran up and down the narrow beach until she was out of breath, then grabbed hold of a tree limb above her head and swung from it. Lucky leaped up and touched her arm with his paws, then dropped down and ran full speed up the river bank.

She heard a child's voice cry out, and, startled, dropped to the ground, her hands still clutching the branch over her head.

"Grampa Gene," the voice said, "there's a dog."

She saw him then, a boy of about nine, in jeans that were wet and plastered to his legs. Just as she saw him, he saw her and took a step backward.

"Grampa Gene," he called out again, "it's Paul Bunyan!"

From a clump of birches near the river a figure appeared, an old man, very small and slightly bent, pulling a child's wagon piled with paper bags and parcels wrapped in brown paper and an old shovel. He wore an ancient yachting cap on his thatch of white hair, and his cotton trousers too were wet.

"Where?" he said, in a surprisingly strong and deep voice.

"Over there."

The old man shaded his eyes and looked at Kitty.

She let go of the branch and it snapped back.

"It's Paul Bunyan," the boy said again.

The old man frowned at him. "That ain't a courteous thing to say, Jody. Where's your manners?"

Jody hung his head. "I'm sorry. It *looked* like . . ."

The man interrupted him. "That's enough of that foolishness." He patted Lucky's head and came toward Kitty. "Afternoon, ma'am. The boy didn't mean to be rude. They just don't think, children don't."

"That's all right," Kitty said. "People are always surprised I'm so big."

"It's useful to be big. I always wished I was myself." He glanced at her wet jeans. "You see how you musta sailed across that river hardly noticing it, while we little fellas got drenched good and proper." He squeezed some water out of his shirt.

"What's your dog's name?" the boy named Jody asked.

"I call him Lucky."

"He's a neat dog."

"He can climb trees."

The boy gave her a skeptical grin. "Aw."

"Honest. You stick around and you'll see."

"Can we travel with 'em, Grampa Gene? I want to see him climb a tree."

The old man looked at Kitty a moment. "Well, now, depends on: a) do they want us, and b) are we traveling the same direction."

"Sure, we want you," Kitty said. "We'd love to

have company. We're heading toward the Maine coast around Ogunquit." There I go again, she thought, trusting people. For all she knew, he might be a detective sent out to find Lucky, or an FBI man after her. But he sure didn't look like it.

"That's our route," the man said. "I'm taking the boy to his aunt in Portland."

The boy looked troubled for a moment. "He wants me to go live with her," he said.

A look of pain crossed the man's face. "It ain't that I want to do it, Jody. You know that." To Kitty he said, "I got to, that's all. I've had the lad since his folks died, back around four years ago, but I've got this heart trouble, and I could kick off any time. Then where'd he be? That's what I had to ask myself."

"I could stay in the cabin," Jody said. "I could make out just fine."

"Know you could," the man said, "but they wouldn't let you. Soon as the school found out I was dead, they'd send social workers and all the like of that, and you'd end up in some foster home, and I don't see no sense that happening when you got a perfectly good aunt that wants you to live with her." To Kitty he said, "His aunt wanted him all along, but the boy was bound and determined to stay with me. We had to get out of sight so's we could swing it."

"Aunt Mary's husband would have gotten a court order," Jody said.

"Well, now they was only doing what they thought

was right. Mary is a good girl, and she'll treat you good, Jody. And she's shed that husband. Got a new one, bound to be nicer. You'll have a new bike and new clothes. . . ."

Kitty could tell they had been through this conversation many times.

"I don't need a bike," Jody said. "And my clothes are okay."

"We ain't told this nice lady our names," the man said. "Where's our manners? I'm Eugene Delaware."

"He's got a state named after him," Jody said.

"Sure have. And this is my grandson, Jody Franklin."

"You've got a famous man named after *you,*" Kitty said.

"I know. Benjamin. He discovered lightning."

"Electricity, boy," Mr. Delaware said. "It was God discovered lightning."

"I'm Kitty LeBlanc," Kitty said. "I'm glad we're going the same way."

The old man sat down abruptly. " 'Scuse me. That old river . . ." He looked pale and fumbled in his shirt pocket for a tiny bottle. "Hope she kept dry." He handed it to Jody, who took out a tiny white tablet and gave it to him.

The old man sat very tense and still, hardly breathing, for about two minutes, and then he relaxed. "That did it. Sorry, ma'am. I got this tricky pump."

"He means his heart," Jody said. "A heart is a

pump, and the arteries are substations, and the veins are little rivers. . . ."

The old man held up his hand. "I doubt Miss Kitty wants a lesson in anatomy, lad."

"That's all right," Kitty said. "I've got a friend that's got high blood pressure and she takes some little pills, too."

The old man brightened. "Is that right? Say, I'd like to meet that lady. I got nobody to talk to about my symptoms, and it spoils half the fun." He got up.

"You better ride awhile, Gramp," Jody said.

Obediently, the old man climbed into the wagon and settled himself among the packages and bags. "We got our worldly goods here."

"Would you like me to pull?" Kitty said.

"Maybe we could harness up Lucky," Jody said.

She smiled. "He's too darned independent. If he saw a squirrel, he'd run off and tip the wagon over." She took the handle, and they started along the path. "Let me know if I bump you too much."

"He don't mind that," Jody said. "He's used to bumps and rolls. He was a fisherman, used to go up to the Grand Banks and get into terrible storms, didn't you, Gramp?"

"Sure did," the old man said serenely.

"We live on his Social Security." The boy skipped alongside of her. He burst out laughing when Lucky came running back along the trail, leaped into the wagon, and sat down in Mr. Delaware's lap.

The old man laughed, too, and put his arms around Lucky. "Well, now you got a full train."

Kitty felt happy, better than she'd felt in a long time. She began to sing "It's a Long Way to Tipperary," and in a moment the boy and the old man joined in.

CHAPTER ELEVEN

KITTY soon realized that Mr. Delaware and Jody were going to slow her down a good deal. When Mr. Delaware got a gray look, Kitty insisted they stop for a few minutes. He wouldn't complain or ask her to rest, but she knew he needed to, and she didn't want the man to have a heart attack out there in the woods. Jody was always glad to stop so he could romp with Lucky, but so far he hadn't been able to coax Lucky up a tree.

"You just keep your eye on him," Kitty said. "Sooner or later up he'll go."

They stopped in late afternoon to make a camp for the night. It was a good deal easier having Mr. Delaware to give advice about shelters and fires, and having Jody as a helper. In no time at all the three of them and the dog were settled into a comfortable little lean-to, and water was heating for coffee. Kitty made tuna fish sandwiches with Myrt's tuna fish and Mr. Delaware's loaf of bread.

There was no wind, but as the sun went down,

they felt a wintry chill in the air. Mr. Delaware shivered and inched closer to the fire. "Winter's in the air."

Jody eyed him critically. "You're looking better, Grampa Gene. Healthier, like."

He smiled. "You and Miss Kitty and that beauty of a dog have perked me up." He tilted his yachting cap forward over his eyebrows, giving himself a jaunty look, and it seemed to Kitty, too, that he did seem younger. She mentioned it.

" 'Mithridates, he died old,' " Mr. Delaware said.

Politely Kitty said, "Was he one of your relatives?"

Jody answered. "He was a real ancient king, back in B.C. times, and in those days people were always killing kings so *they* could be king. They poisoned 'em. So Mithridates was too smart for 'em. He began taking a teeny little bit of poison every day until he built up an imm-m . . ." He looked at his grandfather.

"Immunity."

"Yeah, till he built up that, and when they tried to poison him, he just ate the poisoned food and said, 'Umm, delicious. You must give my wife the recipe.' And he lived to be real old."

"Oh, I see. That was pretty smart."

"See, if you're too stupid or too trusting and you think everybody's good just because you want to think so, you're apt to die young."

"On the other hand," Mr. Delaware said, "some people *are* good. The trick is to learn the difference."

Kitty studied his lined old face. "How does a person learn that, Mr. Delaware?"

For a moment he didn't answer. "That's always kind of a poser," he said finally. "Be a good observer, maybe. In my experience, the ones that are too apt to trust everybody and get their lives all fouled up are the ones that are so wrapped up in themselves, they don't really look around. You know what I mean?"

"I think so."

"A little healthy skepticism never hurt. But don't shut yourself off from goodness and love." He grinned broadly. "Say, don't I sound like Dear Abbie though?"

"My grandpa likes to read poems," Jody said. "He knows a thousand poems by heart."

"Oh, not that many, lad. But on a fishing boat you got a lot of spare time sometimes. Some fellas whittle, some read spy novels, some argue. Me, I like to get a good poem by heart."

"I've never read much poetry," Kitty said.

"It can be a comfort."

Kitty poured the coffee, and Jody was allowed to have some with a generous amount of milk made from Myrt's powder. He sighed happily when he had finished eating. "I wish we could stay right here forever. Never go anywhere."

"It'd get a mite chilly, with winter coming at us," his grandfather said.

"I don't care. I'd build us a real log cabin. I know how. I've read about it. Could we, Gramp?"

"Haven't got an axe." Mr. Delaware stared into the fire as if his mind were far away.

Soon after it was dark, Jody fell asleep, wrapped in one of the old blankets from the cart. Mr. Delaware rummaged in his pockets till he found an ancient pipe and a tobacco pouch. "Ain't supposed to indulge myself in the wicked weed," he said, "but there are times when I go ahead and do it. I don't know if it'll make that much difference in the long run." He sighed. "Or the short run."

Both of them were silent for a while. The fire burned down to a steady glow, and Kitty put on another log that would keep it going through at least part of the night.

"I'm glad we met up with you, Miss Kitty," he said. "It's taken a real load off my mind. But I'm afraid it's going to add one to yours."

"Don't worry about me," she said. "I'm pretty tough."

"Tough and gentle. That's a real good combination." Again he was silent. "To tell you the truth, I'm not sure I'll make it to Portland."

"Oh, sure you will, Mr. Delaware."

He held up his hand. "No, we got to face reality, Miss Kitty. Prepare for trouble, and then it won't throw you off your course when it comes. I've had two of these heart attacks, and the doctor talked real gloomy about if I had another one." With sudden irritation he said, "Some doctors, you think they missed their calling. They're so darned gloomy, they ought to have been undertakers." Then he chuckled. "On the other hand, I've run into undertakers that are so doggone cheerful, they ought to have been used-car salesmen. So there you are. But I was going to say . . ." He tapped the tobacco in his pipe with a sliver of wood and struck another match. "If I was to make the last port while we're still out here in the woods, I want for you, if you please, to bury me where I keel over. I've got a kind of gravestone, made of wood, that I'm working on—hope to get it finished before it's needed. You can just stick it in the ground and leave it at that. And then if you would deliver Jody to his aunt, I can't tell you how much I'd appreciate it." He fished a piece of paper from his pocket and handed it to her. "There's her name and address. She's a good woman, she really is. Maybe don't understand boys too well, but she'll learn." He leaned back, tired.

"Sure, of course I'll do it if it's necessary, but I've got a hunch we're all going to get to Portland just fine." She was not as confident as she sounded, however. Mr. Delaware looked awfully frail and tired. But even if he made it all right, she would see them to the door of this aunt in Portland. It wouldn't take her too much longer.

"You might be wondering," Mr. Delaware said, "why we're hoofing it all that way. I'll tell you why. Three reasons. One is trains and buses, what they like to call public transportation, cost money, and I want to leave whatever little I've got intact for the boy. Second is, if that social worker comes around, she won't have any hint of how we went or where we went. She ain't a bad woman, and she's only doing her job, but she does get mighty aggravating at times with all those questions and all that advice. I never went past high school myself, but I've been around a lot longer than she has. The College of Hard Knocks, that's my college. Then there's the third reason for not using public transportation, and that is that there ain't any. If you want to go east to west or west to east in this neck of the woods, you find your own way to get there. If you want to go north and south, no problem. But I guess you know that, being on foot yourself."

"I guess it's because of the tourists," Kitty said.

"Yep. Ski trains, kids going to camp, all that stuff, they come from the south of us."

He gave a long sigh. "I do hope I make it to the shore. I pine to see open water again. We went inland so as to hide out in case Mary's husband come looking. He was a regular bird dog when he set out to do something. I figured he'd look for us along the shore. I don't care for being landlocked, but I guess it didn't hurt me any. Well, I'll get in a bit of a snooze now, and tomorrow we'll hit for the shore." He curled up like a child on the ground and yawned. " 'An aged man is but a paltry thing, A tattered coat upon a stick unless

Soul clap its hands and sing. . . .' " He opened one eye and looked at her and in a slightly stronger voice he finished. " 'And therefore I have sailed the seas and come to the holy city of Byzantium.' " He sighed and fell asleep.

CHAPTER TWELVE

Snow sifting through the boughs wakened Kitty in the morning. Mr. Delaware was already up, stirring the fire, and Jody was trying to make a snowball. Lucky kept sniffing the snow and then using his front paw to get it off his nose.

"Looks like he's forgotten snow," Mr. Delaware. "How old is he—about a year?"

"About that," Kitty said. "I think." She got up and began to prepare breakfast. At Mr. Delaware's instructions Jody had whittled three long sticks on which he skewered chunks of bread for toasting. Out of the wagon Mr. Delaware brought some bacon and a frying pan. Soon the zestful smells of cooking bacon and coffee cheered them.

In spite of the cold, Kitty felt cheerful. The old man looked brighter, and he whistled as he went about preparing for departure. And both Jody and Lucky were obviously enjoying themselves.

She noticed how helpful Jody was. His grandfather had taught him courtesy and thoughtfulness. She wondered what Mr. Delaware would do if he got to

Portland all right and left Jody. She hated to think of him in an old folks' home or anything like that. On an impulse, she said, "Mr. Delaware, why don't you come stay with my Aunt Lee and me after you leave Jody with his aunt? You could stay with us till you found a place to get settled." She could pay Aunt Lee for his board.

He gave her such a warm smile, she felt almost embarrassed. She was not used to that kind of emotion. "That's about the kindest thing I ever heard," he said, "and I'll bear it in mind, Miss Kitty, I truly will. Did you hear that, Jody? Wasn't that about the kindest thing you ever heard?"

But Jody's face clouded. "I don't see any need for me going to Auntie's house if you're all right. Why can't we just get us another cabin?"

Mr. Delaware patted the boy's shoulder. "Well, well, we ain't going to worry about it today, are we? Say, look at that dog take off, will you? He must have seen a rabbit."

Kitty had to call and whistle for a long time before Lucky came bounding back. "About time," she told him crossly. "You held us up." She was a little worried, now that she had said that to Mr. Delaware about staying at Aunt Lee's. What if Aunt Lee didn't like the idea? She had always been hospitable, though. Kitty could remember her taking in a family whose house had burned one winter, and she always had some cousin or other visiting.

It continued to snow as the day wore on. The snow didn't stick to the ground much, but it made travel difficult. They followed a dirt road for a long time, staying in the tire marks left by an occasional milk truck or logging truck, but everything grew a little soggy, and they had to pull the cart against the drag of the mud. Mr. Delaware walked as much as he could, but now and then he had to give up and rest. Pulling him in the wagon was such slow, tiring work that they decided it was better to take frequent breaks.

Snow seeped down inside their collars, and Kitty's feet were wet and cold. Mr. Delaware and Jody had rubber-soled boots that protected them, but there was no way to keep the east wind from driving the snow into their faces. Only Lucky seemed to go on enjoying the snow, though he too grew tired more often and would sit down in a manner that said, "Not one step more." Part of the time he was allowed to ride on the cart, his front legs splayed out over the tarpaulin that protected the packages of food and clothes that the old man had brought.

At noon they built a fire in the lee of a rocky overhang and had a hot lunch. After a while their dirt road ended in a junction with State Route 111.

"That goes into Biddeford," the old man said. "If I had my little old pickup that I used to have, we could sail right down that highway and be in Portland before you know it."

There was almost no traffic on the road, and they

stayed with it for a while, keeping off to the left side. Once or twice a truck slowed down as if to offer a lift, but then they picked up speed again.

"We look local," Mr. Delaware said, "with the cart and all. We don't look like we're going any place but home."

"I wish we were home." Jody's face was red with cold, and he looked as if he wanted to cry.

The old man stopped and held up his finger, testing the wind. "I got a feeling we might as well hole up somewheres for the night. We ain't making much headway in this weather."

Kitty said, "Why don't I scout ahead a little way and see if there's a motel? There ought to be one on a highway."

"Expensive," Mr. Delaware said.

"I'll pay for it. No, please, I'd like to. I've been sleeping rough for a whole bunch of nights, and I'd like a hot bath and a good bed. I'll get us a couple of rooms." She looked into the woods at the side of the road. "You two get under those trees for shelter, and I'll be right back. Lucky, stay!" She took off down the road at a fast trot. She was worried about Jody as well as Mr. Delaware. Both of them were chilled and exhausted.

It felt good to move fast and unencumbered along the roadside. She wished she could keep on going to Aunt Lee's. If she didn't have Lucky and Mr. Delaware and Jody . . . She stopped herself. What a wicked thing to think! And anyway, not true. If she hadn't found them, her journey would have been so lonely and depressing, she didn't think she could have stood it.

She rounded a curve in the road and saw two motels ahead on opposite sides of the street. She slowed down so she could size them up first. The one on the left looked plainer, older, therefore probably cheaper. She went into the office and rang the bell on the counter. The expression on the face of the woman who came to meet her made Kitty realize that she probably looked like a wild woman.

"Uh . . . would you have two rooms, one for me, one for an old gentleman and his grandson?"

The woman hesitated and then said, "We have some rooms, yes."

"How much are they?"

The woman gave her the price of a single and a double, and Kitty quickly added it up in her head. She could manage that. "We'll take them, please."

The woman looked past her. "Where are the others?"

"They're coming." She felt nervous. Whenever anyone seemed to suspect her of something, even though she might not be sure what it was she was suspected of, she felt guilty.

Still the woman hesitated. "We don't allow any unruly behavior here."

Kitty's eyebrows rose. "Unruly? Oh, no, nobody's going to be unruly. We're too tired." She smiled, wanting the woman to smile back, but there was no response. "Oh," she said, remembering, "I have a dog. Is that all right?"

The woman scowled. "We don't usually take pets. How big is he?"

Kitty measured with her hands. "Not very big. He's a real nice dog."

"Is he house-broke?"

"Oh, sure, yes." He must be, she thought; it had not occurred to her to wonder, but he had behaved all right at Myrt's. "He's a very clean dog." Still hoping to gain some show of friendliness, she said, "He washes himself like a cat."

The woman's expression plainly said, "Don't tell me lies," but she said nothing. She shoved the registration pad at Kitty. "Your friend'll have to register too." She watched closely as Kitty filled out the form. "Put down your car license number."

Startled, Kitty looked up. "I don't have a car."

The woman's suspicions increased. "How'd you get here? There's no bus any more."

"We—I—we're just hiking through."

"Hiking!"

Kitty thought the woman was going to snatch back the registration pad, and unconsciously she leaned the heel of her hand on it. She wanted those rooms so badly, she felt she couldn't bear it if they were turned away. "We aren't going very far," she said. "And like you said, there's no bus."

"Well, all right. Pay in advance." She glanced at Kitty's backpack. "Is that all the luggage you got?"

"Yes." Kitty smiled again without conviction. "You can't take much when you hike." She counted out the money and gave it to the woman, who examined it as if she expected it to be counterfeit.

At last Kitty had the two keys in her hand. "Outside to your left," the woman said indifferently, and left.

Kitty felt like leaping along the road in exultation. A room! A bath! A bed! And Mr. Delaware and Jody could get a real rest, keep warm, eat a hot meal in the tiny fast-food place next door. She broke into a run, her backpack thumping up and down and her hair flying.

CHAPTER THIRTEEN

In the morning they lingered in their rooms until checkout time. Kitty persuaded Mr. Delaware to stay in bed, and she and Jody brought him bacon and toast and hot tea from the restaurant. He looked tiny in the big bed.

"Ain't had such a good night's sleep in a long time," he said. He insisted on paying Kitty for his room. "In the long run it won't make that much difference, and it was worth it, Miss Kitty, it was worth it." He chuckled. "Tell you the truth, it was worth the price just to see that woman's face when Jody and I came along with our cart and old Lucky sitting on top of our goods and chattels. Looked to me like she was going to have a stroke."

Kitty wished they could spend another day in the rooms, just so Mr. Delaware could rest. It seemed to her he was losing strength, cheerful though he seemed. But there was not enough money to stay over and still have some left for future emergencies.

When she returned the keys to the office, the woman was there. "Your dog do any damage?"

Kitty was annoyed, but she answered politely. "No, of course not."

"There's no 'of course not' about it. I know dogs. You hold on just a minute." She picked up the phone and dialed the cleaning woman. "Elva, take a quick look at 103 and 104, see if there's any damage. They had a dog." She waited, eyeing Kitty severely.

I don't have to stay here, Kitty told herself; I've paid my money. But she waited. She was used to being obedient.

"All right," the woman said on the phone. She nodded to Kitty. "She says it's okay."

"I told you it was." Kitty turned away.

"Who's that old geezer anyway? Is he your grandfather?"

Kitty felt her temper rising. "No, he is not my grandfather. He is my friend."

"Pretty weird friend, if you ask me."

"I didn't ask you." One part of Kitty's mind registered surprise at her own courage in answering back, but she was too angry on Mr. Delaware's behalf to check her feelings.

The woman's voice sharpened. "Pretty sassy, aren't you? You tell me it isn't weird, a young girl big as Wilt Chamberlain running around the country with a little bitty old man and a little kid, pulling a kid's wagon? What's in that wagon, I'd like to know? You people been up to something shady? You got a lot of cash you flashed at me last night, big bills. . . ." She reached for the phone again. "I got a mind to call the cops. I can't afford to be giving shelter to suspicious characters."

Kitty felt the rush of blood to her face. She leaned forward, her hands on the counter, and the woman drew back. "If you get the police on us," she said, "I'll personally sue you for . . . for defaming character. Libel. I'll sue you, and it'll ruin your motel."

The woman turned pale, and Kitty realized with a sense of power she had never felt before that the woman was afraid of her. "I mean it," she said, and turned on her heel and strode out of the office.

For a few minutes she felt a glow of elation. She had spoken up. She had stood up for herself. And it had worked.

At least she thought it had worked. As they went along the road, she began to worry. What if the woman did call a cop? They'd be questioned. Mr. Delaware might get into trouble for taking Jody away from school. The cops might know about her trouble with Mort. And there was Lucky. With some surprise she thought, "We really are suspicious characters."

When Jody was out of earshot, she told Mr. Delaware what the woman had said. He chuckled. " 'Course we're suspicious. We do things our own way; that's mighty suspicious. But it might be just as well, Miss Kitty, if we foiled the long arm of the law. Let's get off this road and take to the woods again."

The snow had stopped, and the going was easy.

They made good time until noon, when they halted by a river for lunch.

"If I reckon right, we're in Maine," Mr. Delaware said.

Kitty gave a whoop of joy and leaped up in the air. Lucky raced around her in tight circles, and Jody chased Lucky.

"I thought we'd never make it," Kitty said. "If we're in Maine, it can't be very far."

"Let's have a look at that compass of yours," Mr. Delaware said. "We don't want to start traveling in circles now."

She noticed how badly his hand shook. "We could rest here a while. In fact we could camp here for the night."

"No, sir-ee," he said. "No slacking off when we're into the home stretch." He whacked Jody on the small of his back. "Home port's in sight, lad."

But Jody sobered up at once and wandered off into the trees. The old man watched him go, his face sad.

"I wish he could take it in his stride."

"Change is hard for kids," Kitty said. "And he loves you so much."

The old man's eyes filled with tears, and he shook his head. Then he smiled up at her. " '. . . suffered a sea change,' " he said, " '. . . suffered a sea change . . .' What's that from? I can't place it."

"I don't know," Kitty said. "I'm awfully ignorant about things."

"Well, well, ignorance is the easiest lack to cure that a person has, I guess. You read much?"

"I like to read, but I don't usually have much time."

"Make time. Let other things go. Read—that's where your soul starts blossoming out. You get so you can put words to things, and see what words other people put to things. There's nothing like it."

"I will read," she said. "From now on. I really will."

He nodded. "If you see the boy from time to time, remind him to read too, if you would be so kind."

"I will."

When they were ready to move on, they had the river to cross. Jody reconnoitered downstream and found a place where they could jump from rock to rock and make it most of the way without getting wet. They unloaded the wagon and took the packages across first, and then Kitty carried the wagon. She would have liked to carry Mr. Delaware, but she didn't dare suggest it. He took a long time, resting on the slippery wet rocks and accepting Kitty's outstretched hand each time he leaped to a further place. Jody slipped and went in up to his knees.

They rested again on the other side, and at a little after four o'clock that afternoon Kitty called a halt. Mr. Delaware was looking pale and he had a drawn look around his mouth—what Aunt Lee used to call 'peaked.' She suspected he might be in pain. She persuaded him to sit down in the wagon and give instructions as she and Jody arranged a shelter at the base of a cliff. Then she built up a good fire to dry out Jody's jeans. Mr. Delaware grinned when Jody went behind a boulder to change into dry jeans.

"He's got to the modest stage," he said. "Won't undress even in front of me."

Kitty smiled and thought of her friend Mick, who used to go in the closet and shut the door when she got into her pajamas, on the nights when Kitty stayed overnight. She wondered if Mick missed her. She had begun to realize that she might have been foolish to think that their friendship ended when Mick fell in love with Billy Mitchell. Maybe people could have boy friends and their old friends both. She'd have to ask Aunt Lee how she felt when Kitty's mother got married.

It was a pleasant evening, and while Jody and Lucky romped through the woods, Mr. Delaware got out his pine plaque, his 'tombstone,' and went to work with his knife. In neat letters he had already carved:

EUGENE DELAWARE
born Wiscasset, Maine, 1908.
died, Maine, 198–

And below the dates he was finishing an inscription that read, "He fished the sea."

When Kitty admired the neatness of his carving,

he stopped and pulled a small package from the wagon. "I don't want to be no King Tut," he said, "loading up with earthly treasures for my voyage over yonder, but I'd take it kindly if you'd bury this with me." He took off the wrapping and held up a polished brass clinometer.

"What is it?"

"Clinometer. It tells you when your ship is listing. It's handy when you're taking on cargo and you want to know are you getting it even in the hold." He gave her his sudden shining smile. "I figure one thing I'd like to know is, am I riding steady."

Kitty held the clinometer in her hand, feeling deeply moved. "You must have really loved the sea and boats and all," she said.

"Yep. I did. It's a way of life, you either love it or you can't abide it." He looked off into the trees for a moment. "It's hard to beat that feeling when you stand watch on a clear night, the wind in your face, and the stars so bright and close you feel like you could reach up a hand and swing on 'em the way a boy swings on a willow tree or a birch. You're a free man, and you aren't even thinking the fishing might be poor this time, or the price might have dropped when you get back. None of that enters your mind." He sighed and picked up his knife. "Yep, it's a good life, all right. But a man's health gives out at last."

Kitty wrapped the clinometer carefully and put it in the wagon.

"You ever read Conrad?" Mr. Delaware asked her.

"No."

"He was a sea-going man. He understood what I'm talking about. You read Conrad sometime."

"I will." It occurred to her that there were a lot of very interesting things to do that she had never thought of doing. In school she read what she was told to read, and she liked some of it, but she had never taken a book out of the library in her life except for book reports. There has always been too much on her mind—worry about her father, worry about money, worry about school and Mick and Coach and the team. . . . Aunt Lee used to read to her though, when she went to bed, and she had liked that. *The Wizard of Oz,* that was one story she had liked. "I'm really going to read a lot when I get to Aunt Lee's," she said.

She cooked a casserole with cans of tuna and bread and a white sauce that she couldn't get the lumps out of. "I'm not a good cook."

"You do just fine," Mr. Delaware said. "There's some tea bags in that brown sack, if you want to brew up some tea. The doc took me off coffee, but I always did prefer tea anyway, so I don't feel deprived." He began to whistle as he carved, and Kitty hummed along with him. It occurred to her that they were like a family, a small, contented, self-sufficient family. It was sad that it could last only a short time.

After supper Mr. Delaware lay back on his blanket, facing the fire, and was quiet for a long time. Kitty saw him take one of his little white pills and slip the bottle back into his pocket when Jody wasn't looking.

After Jody had gone to sleep for the night, she lay awake, keeping watch on Mr. Delaware. But in time fatigue overtook her, and she too slept.

CHAPTER FOURTEEN

In the morning Kitty went for a walk to "figure out the lay of the land." She said she wanted to be sure they were going in the right direction, but what she really wanted was an excuse to keep Mr. Delaware where he was for a while longer. It was a warm Indian summer morning, and it would do him good to sit in the sun and rest. She was worried about him, and it was in the back of her mind that if there were a doctor anywhere near, she ought to ask Mr. Delaware to let her bring him, or take Mr. Delaware to see him. It didn't seem right to speak to a doctor unless she had Mr. Delaware's permission, though. She seemed to be making a lot of decisions about other people; she was not used to it, and she was uncertain how far a person could go.

She didn't come to a town, but she did come to a county road that had some signposts. They were indeed in Maine, and going by the road, they would reach the north-south toll road in a short time. Then it was only twenty miles north to Portland. She sat down on a roadside boulder to think. They couldn't attempt the toll road on foot; it was too dangerous with the traffic. She considered the possibility of hitching a ride, but she was pretty sure Mr. Delaware wouldn't like that idea. She wasn't too enthusiastic about it herself, unless some friendly trucker came along. Judging by the truckers she had seen at the café, they were usually pretty good guys. Another twenty-three or four miles was a lot for Mr. Delaware to have to travel, even if they pulled him in the cart.

She had tried not to think about it, but the thought that she might have to deal with his death stayed in the back of her mind and scared her. She had never seen anyone die. Was it awful? Would he have terrible pain? And how could she protect Jody? They seemed like questions too big to answer.

A pickup truck slowed down and gestured an offer of a ride. She shook her head and walked back up the road. She had better go talk to Mr. Delaware and see what he thought they ought to do.

He was sitting up, carving more letters on his grave marker when she returned. He looked quite perky, as if the rest had done him good. She told him what she had discovered, and he thought for a minute.

"I've been studying on this compass of yours," he said, "and what I think we're on here is probably a forest ranger's trail. I suspect it runs kind of parallel to the east-west highway. I'm a little leery of getting out on a road where there's traffic. I suggest we stay on this trail, and keep an eye glued to the compass, and see how we make out. Sooner or later we'll be out of the woods, of course, but there must be some secondary roads running along the shore after we turn north. If there ain't, we can stick to 101. That won't be near so trafficky as the toll road." He paused. "If worst comes to worst, I'm pretty sure there'd be a bus from Biddeford to Portland." He gave Kitty a long look.

She knew he was telling her about the bus in case she and Jody had to travel alone. But you couldn't take a dog on a bus, could you?

They went along the trail in single file, Jody and Lucky ahead, then Kitty pulling the wagon. When the trail narrowed, Mr. Delaware insisted on walking.

Kitty was thinking they must be getting close to the coastal roads, though their progress had been even slower than usual. Twice the wagon had tipped over when the wheels hit tree roots, and they had had to stop and repack it.

Jody and Lucky were out of sight, but she could hear them somewhere ahead. Suddenly she heard Mr. Delaware say, "Hey . . ." and break off. She turned and saw him pitch forward on his face. He lay still.

For a moment Kitty felt paralyzed. She stood looking at the crumpled little figure, unable to move. Then she went to him and turned him over. She felt for his heart and then his pulse, but there was no beat. She put her hand against his mouth to feel for breath, but there was none. Gently she brushed away the pine needles that clung to his forehead. She closed his eyes. Now that it had happened, she felt a great sadness, but she was calm. She straightened up and looked down at him.

"Don't worry, Mr. Delaware," she said softly. "I'll look after Jody. And we'll bury you just like you said." She walked down the trail to find Jody.

The boy and the dog came racing toward her, leaping high over a pile of dead brush, laughing. But as soon as Jody saw Kitty's face he stopped short and said, "Gramp!" Then he ran past her and threw himself on the ground beside his grandfather, his head on the old man's narrow chest.

Kitty stood helplessly behind him, not knowing how to comfort, and then turned away; if it were herself in a situation like that, she would want to be left alone for a few minutes.

She got hold of Lucky and tied him to a tree a little distance away. The dog whimpered and seemed uneasy.

"Be good," she said to him in a low voice. "Don't make a fuss now. Jody is unhappy."

She got the shovel from the wagon and walked away from Jody and his grandfather, looking for a place where she could dig. She wasn't sure how long it took for rigor mortis to set in, but for Jody's sake if nothing else they ought to get this over with. She tried the ground in several places, but it was hard, and there were tree roots under the surface of the soil and pine needles.

Finally she found some sandy ground, and she began to dig. It was hard work, but it was possible. Without a coffin she wouldn't have to dig so very deep. It made her shudder to think that animals would get to him, but if you were dead, something got to you sooner or later—worms and decay and all that. Unless you had yourself mummified.

After a few minutes of digging, she went back to see if Jody was all right. The boy had covered his grandfather with one of the blankets, and he sat beside him with his hand resting on Mr. Delaware's chest. His face was streaked with dirt and tear stains, but he was quiet.

I should have gotten the blanket, Kitty thought. But then maybe it made Jody feel a little better to do something like that.

"I didn't mean to just leave you," she said. "I thought you might want to be alone. I mean the two of you."

Jody nodded. He had a faraway look, as if he were listening to her with only the top of his mind. Twice he sighed a long shuddering sigh, like a sob.

"I found a nice place for the grave," she said. "The ground is dry and sandy, and I can dig it all right without running into roots and things."

Jody sighed again and got up. "I can help dig."

"I was thinking, why don't you cut some nice pine boughs to line the grave with, make it more comfortable like."

"All right." He had a little pile of things neatly arranged beside the body, and from it he picked up Mr. Delaware's knife. "He told me to take the things out of his pockets." He held out an envelope. "There's a letter for my aunt. Explaining."

As he walked away with the knife, she said, "You could take Lucky with you, if you want to. I tied him so's he wouldn't bother you."

Jody untied the dog and knelt beside him for a moment with his arms tight around him. Lucky touched his black nose to Jody's cheek.

For the first time tears welled up in Kitty's eyes, but she turned away and went back to her digging. After the topsoil was tossed aside, the digging was harder, the soil more moist. She took off her sweater and rolled up her sleeves, trying to ignore the blisters that were forming on the palms of her hands. She worked out a counting system, one to bend, two to dig in, three to lift up, four to toss the dirt aside. Sweat ran into her eyes and she had to break her counting more and more often to mop her face with her sleeve. Pain stabbed between her shoulders. Funny, she thought, how you think you're in good shape, and then you find a whole bunch of muscles you haven't used. She gritted her teeth and dug harder as the soil grew heavier.

It seemed like hours before she got even a shallow grave. Jody had brought great armfuls of pungent-smelling pine, and when the grave was deep enough, they lined it carefully on the bottom and the sides, leaving some for the top. She eased her shoulders into a more comfortable position, and let Jody do the work with the pine. It was better for him to keep busy.

He cried out in protest when Lucky leaped into the grave. "Don't do that! That's for Grampa Gene."

Kitty caught the dog and tied him up again, but he wailed his mournful cry until neither of them could stand it. Kitty scolded him and took him some distance away where, although they could still hear him clearly, it was not quite so nerve-wracking.

It was time to put Mr. Delaware in his grave. Kitty lifted the blanket-wrapped body, light as a child's, and carried it to the grave. Seeing the look on Jody's face, she said, "Why don't you go see if you can hush Lucky? Take him for a little walk."

He turned to go, but then came back. "No, I want to be here."

"You're sure?"

He nodded. "I've thought about it a whole lot."

"All right. Will you get the clinometer out of the wagon?"

While he went to get it, she lowered the body into the grave. She hadn't realized how small Mr. Delaware really was. It was like lifting little Timmy Prentiss onto his bunk after he'd fallen asleep. When Jody came back with the clinometer, she let him place it on his grandfather's chest. The boy tucked the blanket carefully around the old man's feet, and still crouching beside the grave, he looked up at Kitty, his blond hair falling almost into his eyes. She would have to get his hair cut, Kitty thought, before she took him to his aunt.

"He ought to have some nice boughs on top," he said.

"All right." She waited while the boy picked out some especially well-shaped branches and laid them gently on top of the blanket.

It was time to fill the grave. She picked up the shovel and looked at Jody. "Honest, why don't you do something about Lucky? When it's time for you to put the headstone in, I'll call you." She couldn't bear to throw dirt on Mr. Delaware with Jody watching.

He hesitated, looked at the grave a moment longer, and then turned away. In a minute Kitty realized that Lucky had stopped howling. She worked fast, wanting to get the job done before Jody came back. It wasn't hard, but it made her feel terrible to be shovelling dirt on top of that sweet old man. Although she was hardly aware of them, tears streaked her face.

She was just finishing when Jody came back with Lucky on the rope. He got the wooden marker from the wagon and opened his grandfather's knife.

"He didn't get it quite done." He sat down on the ground and with his mouth held tight, he carved out the letters *e* and *a* in "sea" and finished the date.

"It ain't as neat as Gramp's."

Kitty looked at it. "I think it's fine. You put it in the ground now."

He spent some time deciding on the exact spot, and finally he thrust the bottom of the marker into the soft dirt. He took it out again and got the shovel.

"It's got to be so it'll stay." He dug down a way in the dirt at the head of the grave, positioned the marker, and tapped it down with the back of the shovel. "Is it straight?"

"Tips a little to the left."

"Now?"

"Perfect." She looked down at the slightly raised shape of the grave, wishing she had her kayak to put over it. "Listen," she said, "how about if we put the wagon upside-down over the grave?"

He thought about it. "Like a little house."

"Yes."

They unloaded the wagon, which contained much less than it had originally, most of the food having been eaten, and they turned it over and placed it lengthwise on the grave, the handle extending along the soft dirt. Jody brought some heavy rocks to hold it in place.

He stood back and looked at it. Softly he said, "Good. It'll keep out the rain." He looked up at Kitty. "You ought to say something, you know, like ministers do at the cemetery."

She felt panicky. No words came to her. But he was right, something should be said. For a minute she stood looking at the marker, and then she said, "Please, God, take good care of Mr. Delaware, who was a fisherman and a kind and loving man. I am his friend, Kitty

LeBlanc, and this is his grandson, Jody Franklin, who loves him very much, and we ask You to look after him, for Jesus Christ's sake, Amen."

Jody took a long, quivering breath and turned away. He picked up the things that had been in the wagon and put them in the blanket, making a pack, and he started down the trail without looking back.

Kitty said, "Good-bye, Mr. Delaware. Don't worry, I'll look after him."

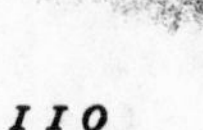

CHAPTER FIFTEEN

IT WAS late afternoon when they reached the sea. Kitty had let Jody set the pace, and the boy had moved along at a fast clip, silent and frowning. Kitty tried once or twice to get him to give up the pack he had fashioned out of the blankets, but he insisted on carrying it over his shoulder, gypsy-fashion.

When they came to the toll road, Kitty put Lucky on the rope, and they crossed it still heading east. Kitty had decided to take Jody to Aunt Lee's for the time being. It was too much to ask him to go directly to his aunt's so soon after the shock of his grandfather's death. Also she realized that she hated to part with him. He had agreed, with obvious relief, to her plan.

"Will she mind?"

"Aunt Lee? Oh, no. She'll be glad to see you."

At the beach they stopped and stared with pleasure at the sparkling sea. Except for a couple walking hand in hand, and some fishermen on the nearby pier, there were no people in sight. Most of the summer cottages were closed. Kitty took Lucky off the rope and let him race up and down in the soft sand. He came running back to them with sand all over his nose, and for the first time since early morning Jody smiled.

Kitty had a churning excitement in her stomach. They were so close now! It almost seemed that she recognized this beach, but she couldn't be sure of that. Beaches often looked alike until you got to know them very well. But it gave her a sense of home.

Left to herself she would have pushed on, tired though she was, but she could tell that Jody was exhausted. She left the boy and the dog and walked up the beach to the nearest town to see what the possibilities were. For one thing she had to find either a map or some road signs. She thought they were north of Aunt Lee's place, because they had been following Mr. Delaware's plan to head for Portland. She didn't want to go galloping off in the wrong direction.

She came to a Chamber of Commerce booth where a friendly woman gave her a map and confirmed her feeling that the direction she needed to go was south. She asked about buses and found there was not another one until morning, and that no, the lady thought, they would not allow dogs. She smiled at Kitty.

"Sounds unfriendly to us dog lovers, doesn't it, but I guess they have to have their rules." She looked at Kitty a moment and then said, "If you were to need a ride badly, you could ask the police. They're pretty good about that, if it's kind of an emergency. You look tired."

For a moment Kitty thought longingly of a fast,

comfortable police car speeding them to Aunt Lee's, but then she knew there would be questions. "Oh, thank you," she said, "I'm okay. Thanks just the same, though."

She left quickly. There were three motels along the road, and several restaurants and gas stations. Mentally, she added up the money she had left and decided to approach the least elegant-looking of the motels. It was called I-A Economy Motel, which sounded promising. Remembering her last experience, she stopped at a gas station ladies' room to wash her hands and face and comb her hair.

The motel clerk, a young man, paid little attention to her beyond saying that they did have a room with a bed and a cot, and dogs were allowed if they didn't bark. She paid for the room and went back to get Jody and Lucky.

Jody was lying full length on the sand with his head on his arms, and Lucky lay between the boy's feet, his chin on Jody's leg. Lucky ran to greet her, but it was several minutes before Jody responded. She thought at first that he was asleep, but he was not.

"It's a nice motel, no mean old woman this time. You don't mind, do you, if we have beds in the same room?" She was remembering what Mr. Delaware had said about Jody's modesty.

Jody shook his head indifferently. "Doesn't matter."

But when they got to the room, she was careful to

stay away until Jody had had time to take a shower and change his clothes. She took Lucky for a walk along the road, stopping to look in the windows of gift shops and grocery stores. She felt as if it had been years since she had been in a real town. She kept looking for something nice to buy Mrs. Myrt, but she didn't see anything that seemed quite right. In a drugstore she bought some postcards. Maybe later she could send one to Mick and one to Joe.

She and Jody ate at a McDonald's, watched TV awhile, and went to bed early. She was awakened during the night by the quiet sound of Jody's sobbing. She lay awake wondering what to do. Would he mind having her know he cried? He had been so brave all day. But the desolate sobs upset her so much that she finally spoke to him.

"Jody?"

For a moment he didn't answer. "Yeah?" he said at last.

"Are you all right?"

"Sure."

"Can I get you anything? Are you hungry or thirsty or anything?"

"No, I'm okay." His voice sounded choked.

She lay still, suffering from her own inadequacy. What a stupid question! "Can I get you anything?" All that he wanted was his grandfather, and nobody could get him that. It wasn't fair that kids had to feel so bad. She lay awake until at last she heard his regular breathing and knew he was asleep. Poor little boy, poor little boy. She pulled Lucky close to her and finally slept.

In the morning Jody was pale and quiet but composed. They had breakfast at McDonald's and came back to check out. Kitty looked at the telephone a long time, trying to get up her courage to call Aunt Lee, but she couldn't make herself do it. Telephones always made her nervous, and now especially she couldn't face it. Much better just to arrive. If Aunt Lee wasn't home, they would just sit on the porch and wait.

Before they left, she tried to get Jody to go for a swim in the pool in his shorts, but he was shocked at the idea. A person went swimming in swim trunks.

"Well, we'll have to buy you some trunks," she said. "There's a terrific beach just a couple of blocks from Aunt Lee's." She caught his sidelong glance and read his mind. He was wishing he could stay with Aunt Lee and her, not go to Portland at all. She wished it herself. But it wasn't what Mr. Delaware had said to do, and she couldn't ask so much of Aunt Lee.

They left the road and walked back along the beach.

"Does your Aunt Lee have a husband?" Jody asked her.

"She had one a long time ago, when I was a baby, but he died."

"Aunt Mary's 'sposed to have a new one. She divorced the old one. We read it in the paper. Uncle Horace, he was a jerk."

"Maybe the new one is nice."

"I doubt it."

She was sorry it had come up. Jody retreated into a gloomy silence again. But suddenly she grabbed his arm and said, "Look!"

Lucky had run ahead of them and veered off toward a shuttered cottage, where several wind-stunted pine trees provided a windbreak. He leaped up the trunk of the largest tree and out onto one of the branches, where he crouched, looking down at the delighted Jody.

"He did it!" Jody called back to Kitty. "He really did it."

"I told you."

They watched. In a minute Lucky moved and then pulled back his paw in annoyance as pine needles pricked him. He ran a short distance down the trunk, leaped to the ground and sat in front of Jody, looking up at him for approval.

Jody scooped him up in his arms. "That was terrific. Really great. I wish Grampa Gene could have seen that." He hugged Lucky tight and then put him down. "That was really something. I can hardly believe it."

Kitty was pleased that Lucky had performed for Jody. "Good dog. Good boy." He really was the nicest dog she had ever known. She hoped no one ever took him away from her, and that he lived to be a hundred.

A little later she really did begin to recognize landmarks. "Look," she told Jody excitedly, "I used to go fishing from that pier. Aunt Lee used to take me out with some friends of hers to look for lobsters. One of them had lobster pots."

Jody pointed to a half-dozen lobster pots on the pier. "I know them. Gramp had some when we still lived on the sea. I think my father had lobster pots, too." He frowned. "It's hard to remember them." Suddenly frightened, he grabbed her hand. "Will I forget Grampa Gene?"

"No, no, of course you won't."

"But I hardly remember my mother and father. I *remember* them, but they don't seem real."

"Your grandfather will always seem real because you're older. Little kids forget things pretty fast, but not when a person is as old as you are."

"Honest?"

"Honest. It's true, Jody."

Slightly reassured, he let go of her hand. After a while he said, "What else do you see that looks like you remember it?"

"The rocks," she said. "Those are special rocks. You can find the weirdest things in tidal pools in between those rocks."

"Let's look." He ran ahead of her, and they spent a quarter of an hour looking for crabs and jelly fish and anything else the tide had washed in. Now that they were so close to Aunt Lee's, she delayed their arrival. She was scared. What if Aunt Lee said, "Go away"?

What if she had moved? Died? Heard about Mort? What if the cops were waiting? She had to get a firm hold on herself not to panic and run.

But at last she stood up and said, "Well, we'd better go." She brushed the sand from her clothes and strode off down the beach.

CHAPTER SIXTEEN

THE gray shingled house with its faded blue shutters stood on a knoll facing the sea, the front yard still colorful with dark purple asters. Kitty caught her breath and stood still. It was like coming upon a dream and finding it real. She had seen this house so often, sleeping and waking, in her mind's eye, that she had almost forgotten it was substantial and real. She broke into a run up the last stretch of road and over the paving stones of the front walk. She ran up the steps, hearing the clunk of her feet on the old boards, half expecting the blue door to be flung open before she reached it.

But the door remained closed, and although she rang the bell and knocked repeatedly, no one came.

"She isn't home," Jody said. He sat on the step, easing his pack to the porch floor. "She went to buy the groceries or something."

Kitty felt panicky. Aunt Lee *had* to be here. She knocked again, so hard that the panes in the front windows shook.

"Don't break the door down," Jody said. "She

ain't there unless she's deaf."

"She's not deaf." Kitty was fighting the urge to burst into tears. She had come all this way, *all this way,* and Aunt Lee wasn't here. It was more than she could bear.

Finally she sank down on the porch steps, trying to be reasonable. "She'll be along pretty quick. She didn't know we were coming, after all." She couldn't stand it to see her own disappointment reflected in Jody's face. "Don't worry."

"I'm not worrying." But he obviously was. He kept looking up the street. "What does she look like?"

Kitty tried to remember exactly. "She's about five feet three . . ." It struck her that Aunt Lee would look very tiny. Before, she had seemed tall.

"Is she fat?"

"No, no. She's nice and slim, a real pretty lady. She's got blonde curly hair—no, not exactly blonde, more light brown. And kind of golden-brown eyes. She smiles and laughs a lot."

"She sure sounds nice," Jody said wistfully. Then after a minute he said, "But if she ain't fat, she's not that lady that's coming around the house."

Kitty looked. A woman who seemed vaguely familiar was approaching them.

"Kitty?" the woman said. "Kitty LeBlanc?"

"Mrs. Haraden!" Kitty remembered. She was the lady who lived across the lane. She jumped up and heard Mrs. Haraden gasp. "I'm Kitty."

"My goodness! Your aunt said you'd have changed a lot, but I wasn't expecting . . . well, how *are* you? It's good to see you." She gave Kitty a hug, exuding a smell of soapy dishwater and cooking. "Oh, my land o' Goshen, I hardly come above your waist. Child, how tall are you?"

Kitty was too relieved to see Mrs. Haraden to feel self-conscious. "Around five eleven, I guess, unless I've grown in the last few weeks. I probably have."

"My goodness gracious!" Mrs. Haraden stood with her hands on her plump hips. "If Lee hadn't told me to be on the lookout for you, I'd never have dreamed . . ." She beamed at Jody. "Last time I saw this child she was about your size, young fella."

"Aunt Lee knew I was coming?" Kitty felt a surge of fear. The cops?

"Yes, your dad called her. Said you took off without a word, and he was worried 'bout you. Lee said she knew you'd come straight here if you was in trouble."

"Did he . . . did my father say anything about trouble?"

Mrs. Haraden gave her a shrewd look, but she only said, "Not that I know of, except he was having an attack of the guilties, and had had a little too much out of the bottle. You know how Clarence is." Then she laughed. "I guess you do, and that's why you're here." She smiled at Jody again. "Where did you come from, young fella? That's a pretty little dog you got there."

"Oh, this is my friend Jody Franklin," Kitty said. "Jody, say hello to Mrs. Haraden."

"Hello," Jody said.

"Look, here's Lee now." Mrs. Haraden stood on tiptoe and waved wildly as an old model Plymouth turned into the drive and stopped.

Kitty was almost afraid to look. But it was Aunt Lee, sure enough, wearing a blue denim skirt and a navy jacket and looking the same as ever. She left the car door open and ran to Kitty with her arms spread wide.

"Kitty, Kitty, Kitty, I can't believe it." She hugged her and kissed her and hugged her again, half crying. "My dear Kit. After all this time. Oh, Beulah, isn't she a beauty!"

"Fine-looking girl." Mrs. Haraden beamed at them, and then said reluctantly, "Well, I'd best be going."

"Stay for a cup of tea, Beulah."

"No, no. You two got a lot to talk about. I'll see you later." She leaned down and patted Lucky, who peered at her with his puzzled, inquisitive look. "You're some dog, you are."

As if she were not in the least surprised to find Kitty accompanied by a small boy and a dog, Aunt Lee herded them all into the kitchen, made tea for Kitty and herself, hot chocolate for Jody, and poured some milk in a saucer for Lucky. Then she sat down and said, "Now tell me everything."

A little later when Jody and Lucky had gone down to explore the beach, Kitty talked more freely, both about her own problems and about Jody's. Somehow she had expected Aunt Lee to provide instant solutions for everything, but she only listened attentively and said little.

Once the telephone rang, and after she had hung up, Kitty said, "Do you think my father will call again?"

"I doubt it. I told him I had not seen you nor heard from you and had no expectation that you would come here. He seemed to accept that."

"How . . . how did he seem?"

"Rather subdued for Clarence. Almost polite." She laughed. "Your dad and I were never bosom friends, you know."

"Did you mind when he married Mom?"

"Oh, I hated it. I thought I'd lost my best friend forever. But that's nonsense, of course. I think we were even closer after she got married. It was different, but deeper."

Kitty thought about that for a minute. She must send that postcard to Mick before she forgot it. "And he didn't say anything about Mort."

"No. I think you should put that out of your head. If that miserable fellow had died or even been seriously hurt, I'm sure there'd have been all kinds of a hue and cry, and you'd surely know about it." She got up and began preparations for a fish chowder. "But there's an easy way to clear your mind."

Kitty looked at her. "You mean call him up?"

"Yes. But it's for you to decide. He came after you once, and he might again, but you're almost grown up now. You can stand on your own feet."

"Yes," Kitty said, with a stirring of surprise. That was what she had begun to do; that was why she felt so different. All her life she had done what she was told, and left the rules and decisions to other people. Now she had begun to take charge of her own life, and that meant she was turning into a real person. "I'll call him later."

But she put it off that night, and she put off any moves concerning Jody. She ought to call his aunt, let her know what had happened; but he had begun to relax, even to laugh occasionally, as he romped with Lucky and talked to Aunt Lee and curled up with a plate of cookies in front of the television. She didn't have the heart to upset him.

Things went on as they were until Saturday afternoon. Aunt Lee was working at the library, and Jody and the dog were hunting for starfish. Kitty ate a second piece of Aunt Lee's good chocolate cake and stared at the telephone.

When she had finished the cake and washed the plate and swept up the crumbs, she picked up the phone and dialed her home number. It rang three times, and she thought with relief, "He's not home," but just as she started to hang up, she heard her father's voice saying, "Hello? hello?" in that impatient, suspicious way he had, as if he expected some hostile force to be on the other end.

"Hi, Pop." Her voice sounded strained. She cleared her throat. "Hello, Dad, this is Kitty."

After a moment of silence he said, "Well, I didn't think it was Queen Elizabeth. Where in hell are you?"

"I'm fine," she said, as if she had misunderstood him. "I wanted to let you know I'm just fine."

"About time you called. I suppose you're at Lee's. She swore you weren't, but . . ."

"I wasn't. I've just got here."

"Well, when you coming home? I 'spose Mort and I can drive the pickup over to get you. You're supposed to be in school, you know. When you want to come?"

She gripped the back of the chair for support. "I'm not coming home."

There was a silence. "Not coming home?"

"No. I've left home, Dad."

"I didn't give my permission."

"I'm sorry, but I'm almost grown-up, you know. I'll be fifteen next week."

"You're still a minor. I got rights . . ."

Her voice strengthened. "You don't have rights to me, Dad. I'm a separate human being."

His voice changed. "You ain't mad about Mort, are you? I mean you wouldn't bring charges or nothing like that? He was just being friendly."

She almost laughed. He'd asked if *she* was going to

bring charges! "No, I'm not going to bring charges. But he wasn't being friendly, and I'm never coming back."

"All right, all right, but you mind what Lee tells you. Don't get too uppity just because you're bigger'n anybody on God's green earth. You're still a minor, and I'm your father."

She recognized the bluster for what it was. "Take care of yourself, Dad. I'll stay in touch." She hung up and sat down heavily on the kitchen chair. Her legs felt hollow. She was free of her father. She had simply told him she wasn't coming home, and that was that. She wanted to howl with joy, but she was afraid she would alarm Mrs. Haraden, who was out in front of her house burning leaves.

Kitty cut herself another piece of cake and sat with her long legs sprawled out in front of her, not even caring that she spilled crumbs. She could sweep them up, couldn't she? Nobody would scream at her.

In a few minutes the phone rang, and her old fears revived. She didn't answer, but it rang again and again, and she was afraid not to answer; it might be Aunt Lee wanting something.

"Hello?" She held the receiver a little away from her.

"Kitty?"

"Joe!" Her self-confidence surged back. "Joe, is it you?"

"Sure is, Kit. Your old man just told me you

called. He said you're not coming home."

"That's right. I'm staying with Aunt Lee."

"Well, I miss you, but all I can say is, hallelujah. Listen, Kit, I've got news."

"What?"

"That buddy I sent your tapes to, remember?"

"Sure."

"I heard from him."

Kitty laughed. "Did he tell you to forget it?"

"I'll read you the letter. Hold on a second."

She heard the rustle of paper and then his voice again.

"Dear Joe: Good to hear from you. How's the missus and the hot dog business et cetera. Sometimes I wish I were in the hot dog business myself. You need a good salad man? Anyway I got the tapes you sent, and I'll lay it on the line. I know you know I wouldn't give you any b.s., and that's why you sent them to me, right?"

He paused, and Kitty thought, "All right, here we go."

"I think your young friend Kitty is a very talented kid. You say she's fourteen, and I am amazed that she has so much richness and power. Is she a big kid, by any chance? Big or little, she's got to be encouraged. Her voice is uneven and of course she has no technique, but she's got a quality that reminds me of that English singer, Kathleen Ferrier." Joe paused, and said, "What'd I tell you, Kit." He went on reading. "I don't know any voice teachers in your neck of the woods, but when she gets out of high school, let me know. I think they have scholarships at Juilliard and I'll do what I can to help. Take care and let me hear from you. I'm really interested in Kitty LeBlanc. Yours, Angelo."

There was a silence on the line and then Joe said, "Well, Kit, what do you think of that?"

"Gosh," she said. "Are you sure he means it?"

"Old Angelo wouldn't con me. He means it all right. Now, listen. I think it's better you don't have voice lessons till you're through high school and can go to New York, where they'll teach you right. You've got two more years, right?"

"Right." The conversation seemed unreal.

"Okay. I'm putting away something every month in the Kitty fund, so we'll be ready." He laughed. "The Kitty kitty."

"New York is expensive. I mean even to go there."

"This is my investment in the arts."

"Oh, Joe. Listen, I'll save what I can."

"I know you will, kid. Look, I got a buddy in the restaurant business in Wells. He owes me a favor. I'll call him and see if he can give you a job after school. You could get to Wells, couldn't you?"

"Oh, sure. I could get a second-hand bike. Anyway there's probably a bus." She felt dazzled. She had never taken Joe seriously when he talked about her career. "How can I thank you?"

"By working hard. And getting me a good seat at your concerts."

"My concerts?" She saw herself on a stage in front of a mass of faceless people. "Joe, will they teach me not to be scared?"

"They'll help. But knowing you can do it, that'll be the best help."

"I'll probably trip and fall on my face on my very first entrance."

"Then pick yourself up and go right on. Listen, I'll call you back as soon as I get through to my chum in Wells, all right?"

"How can I thank you?" she said again.

"You just take yourself seriously. You're an artist. Write that on your mirror and say it to yourself every day. That's how to thank me."

After he had hung up, she began to be excited. It was beginning, just beginning, to seem real and possible. She grabbed a sweater and ran out of the house, banging the screen door. She ran at full speed down the beach until she came upon Jody and Lucky. They had found a green crab and were examining it.

"Look," Jody said, "it's got yellow spots. Ain't he pretty?"

Kitty felt so happy, she though she would explode. She grabbed up Lucky and swung him around. "You are the dog of a famous singer," she said. "You are the dog of a singer who is a very talented kid. Got a quality like Kathleen Ferrier, she has." Lucky squirmed, and she put him down.

"What are you raving about?" Jody said.

"I'm going to be a big singer." In full voice she sang the scale up and down again.

He grinned. "You're already a big singer. Are you really going to be a singer? Like on the television?"

"I'm going to give concerts in New York. You can have front row seats. Kitty LeBlanc takes care of her friends."

Jody knelt beside the tidal pool, looking up at her with troubled gray eyes. "Let me stay with you, Kitty, please? Don't send me away."

She dropped to the sand beside him and put her arm around him. "Jody," she said. "Jody."

He leaned against her and was quiet for a long time.

CHAPTER SEVENTEEN

JODY sat huddled on the back seat of Aunt Lee's car, clutching Lucky close to his chest. Kitty sat in front, swiveled around so she could keep an eye on Jody. They had had some long talks, first Kitty with Aunt Lee, then Kitty and Jody.

"He's a darling little boy," Aunt Lee had said, "and as far as I'm concerned, I'd love to keep him here. I just wonder if in the long run it would be the right thing to do. But it's your decision to make, Kitty."

Kitty had not slept well. In the middle of the night she got up and tried to write down in separate columns the reasons for keeping Jody and not keeping Jody. She meant to think about it objectively, but she couldn't stop the tears that fell onto the paper. How, she thought, do unwed mothers stand it to give away their babies. But perhaps that was different, because although the baby would be the girl's own flesh and blood, she wouldn't have got to know him as a person. Jody seemed like Kitty's own family. Jody and Lucky and Kitty . . . it was a unit.

But. There were the arguments against. No matter

what Aunt Lee said, it wouldn't be easy for her to have a young boy in the house. She had taken care of Kitty, but Kitty was a girl, and Kitty was her best friend's child. Jody, after all, meant nothing to Aunt Lee. And there was the expense. She couldn't expect Aunt Lee to support Jody, and even with a job at Joe's friend's place the only way she could make enough, herself, for the two of them was to leave school, pretend she was old enough, fake an I.D. or something. It would be eight or nine years before Jody would be through school himself. And by that time her chance for a career as a singer would be past. Joe would be disappointed, and so would she.

And there was Mr. Delaware's request that she take Jody to his aunt. He had said, "Mary is a good girl." It was Jody's own family. There was a man to help bring up Jody.

Finally, after a long and tearful talk with Jody, they had decided to go and see Aunt Mary. She agreed that if Jody was miserable, she would take him home again. Or if Aunt Mary showed signs of not wanting him, though that seemed unlikely, since she had wanted him before. Kitty called her and in a carefully worded speech, rehearsed ahead of time, she said that Mr. Delaware had died, and that he had thought she would want to see Jody. "He's fine here with us," Kitty said, "with my aunt and me, but we thought you would want to know . . ."

The woman had interrupted. She had a soft, quick voice, and she sounded nervous. "Oh, please bring him here. I want so much to see him. I've worried . . . although I knew Uncle Gene loved Jody so, and he's always been good about sending me pictures of Jody, but I never knew exactly where they were. Can you come tomorrow?"

So Aunt Lee was driving them to Cape Elizabeth, just south of Portland, where Jody's aunt lived.

Aunt Lee made easy conversation from time to time, but it was hard for Kitty to answer, and Jody said nothing at all.

When they turned into the street where his aunt lived, he pulled his grandfather's yachting cap down over his forehead and buried his face in Lucky's shoulder.

"I'll do some shopping and come back in about twenty minutes," Aunt Lee said. "Is that all right?"

Kitty nodded and opened the door for Jody. He held the new leash that Aunt Lee had bought for Lucky, and he had his clothes and things in an old flight bag that she had found for him. He hung back a few steps behind Kitty as they went up the steps of the white clapboard house.

"Look, it's got a nice backyard," Kitty said, but Jody didn't look up.

Before she could lift the brass knocker, the door opened and a woman of about forty faced them. She was tanned and rather pretty, with short curly gray hair and gray eyes like Jody's. She wore a brown linen dress and sandals.

"Mrs. Ellicott?" Kitty wasn't sure it was Jody's aunt; she had not expected anyone so—she wondered what she *had* expected—auntlike? Somehow she had had the impression of an older woman, more like the person on the Mrs. Butterworth syrup bottle.

"Yes." The woman smiled uncertainly, and her voice was breathless. She looked past Kitty at Jody. "Jody . . ." She raised her arm as if to embrace him, then checked the gesture.

One mark for her, Kitty thought. She knows enough not to embarrass him with a lot of slobbery emotion.

Slowly Jody raised his head. "Hi," he said.

"Come in, come in, both of you. Is that your dog?" she said to Kitty. "He's a basenji, isn't he?"

Kitty followed her into the hall. It was an attractive house, clean and comfortable-looking. "Yes, most people don't know what kind he is."

"I love dogs. I used to go to every dog show for miles around. I lost my poodle a few months ago." She smiled at Jody. "If you like dogs, we'll have to get one right away."

"Poodle?" The scorn in Jody's voice was unmistakable.

His aunt flushed. "Well, Jasper was a standard

poodle, not one of the fancy little ones. But we can get whatever you want. Would you like a dog?"

Jody looked at Lucky with such love and sadness, Kitty thought she would burst into tears. "No," he said, "not now, thanks."

They sat down in the living room, Lucky held close to Jody's feet, though he plainly wanted to explore.

"Look at that neat ship model," Kitty said to Jody, trying to break some of the strain.

He glanced at it. "Yeah."

"My husband made it," the woman said. "He loves boats. Do you like boats, Jody?"

"Sure." His tone indicated that it was a stupid question.

Kitty felt desperate. They couldn't go on sitting here, that poor woman so nervous she could fly, and Jody making unkind answers. "Look," she said, "why don't you take Lucky for a walk in the backyard? He had to sit still all the way over." To the woman she said, "Would that be all right?"

The woman reacted with relief. "That's fine." She went to a glass door leading off the room. "Jody, your uncle Pete is out there in the boathouse. He stayed home today, and he's painting the dory. He's anxious to meet you."

They both stood in the doorway for a moment, watching Jody's tense back as he trudged along the garden path with Lucky pulling at the leash.

"He doesn't want to come here, does he?" Mrs. Ellicott looked as if she might burst into tears.

Gently Kitty said, "It isn't that. He wants his grandfather to be alive again. And nobody can fix that."

The woman sat down, linking her fingers together. "I've wanted him for so long. Especially since I married Peter. He would give anything to have a boy."

Kitty said what she had rehearsed. "If it's hard for you, now that you're remarried and all, my aunt and I would love to keep him."

Mrs. Ellicott looked at her with a worried frown. "I haven't asked how you knew them. Are you from their town?"

Kitty had rehearsed that too, but she found she couldn't tell this woman anything but the truth. When she had finished, Mrs. Ellicott sighed. "Think of Uncle Gene coming on foot like that. I'd have been so happy to come get them."

"He liked to do things independent," Kitty said.

"I know." She smiled for the first time. "We had quite a spat when my sister died. I wanted Jody then, but Uncle Gene wanted to bring him up. I must say, he's done a good job. Jody looks fine."

"He's a wonderful boy. He's not being very polite right now, but that's because he's so upset." She looked out the window. "Is that your husband?"

A man in shorts and a white sweatshirt was leaning down patting Lucky and talking to Jody.

Mrs. Ellicott brightened a little. "Yes, that's Pete. He's a very fine man."

Jody and Lucky and the man disappeared into the boathouse.

"He wants to take him sailing. He even talked about buying him a little catboat, but I said not to make too many plans. Some boys don't like boats."

"Oh, Jody likes boats all right. He's like Mr. Delaware."

Mrs. Ellicott looked up at Kitty. "Tell me the truth, Miss LeBlanc, could Jody be happy here? I want him so much, it's hard to even think of not keeping him, but if he's going to be miserable. . . ."

It was Kitty's chance. She could say that perhaps he should stay with Aunt Lee and her for a while. She looked out at the garden. Mr. Ellicott and Jody came out again, Lucky leaping along in front of them. Mr. Ellicott had a basketball in his hands, which he gave to Jody, and after a moment of hesitation Jody tossed it at a basket that was attached to the wall of the boathouse. It missed. She saw the flash of white teeth as Mr. Ellicott laughed, caught it, and tossed it back to Jody. He demonstrated the proper stance, and held Jody by the hips, positioning him for the throw. The ball went into the basket, and Jody turned toward Mr. Ellicott with a pleased smile.

"Pete put up that basket and bought the ball this morning," Mrs. Ellicott said. "He thought Jody might like it."

"I think Jody will love it here," Kitty said quietly.

"Do you really?" The woman's face lit up, and she looked suddenly younger. "Oh, do you? I'll do everything I can . . . Pete says I'm house-proud, but I will not nag Jody, I really won't. Boys can't be expected to keep a house the way a fussy woman would. I promise I won't nag."

"Jody is very neat, I think. Mr. Delaware taught him to be. Mrs. Ellicott, will it be all right if I come to see him now and then?"

"I want you to. Please come often. It will make it easier for Jody. I can tell that he loves you. He trusts you."

Kitty's eyes filled with tears and she turned away. "I'd better be going. My aunt will be coming for me. . . ."

"Miss LeBlanc, you wouldn't consider selling your dog, would you? Jody seems to love him so much. I know basenjis are valuable. We'd be glad to pay whatever you ask."

"You keep Lucky. No, I won't sell him, but you keep him. He was lost, and I found him. I—Please tell Jody I'll call him up tonight. Tell him I'll come to see him real soon." She went to the door.

"You've been so good," Mrs. Ellicott said.

Kitty hurried to Aunt Lee's car and got in. Aunt Lee gave her hand a quick squeeze and said, "We're going to have a shore dinner at the best place in town. And after that I want you to see a gift shop I know about, where you might find something for your friend Mrs. Myrt."

"Right," Kitty said. "Fine." She swallowed hard. "That'll be dandy."